"There is lots of room here. There's a guest room."

Logically, Jessica knew she could not stay. But it felt so good to be here. It felt oddly like home to her, even if it didn't to Kade. Maybe it was because she was aware that for the very first time since she had been attacked in her business, she felt safe.

And so tired. And relaxed.

Maybe for her, home was where Kade was, which was all the more reason to go, really.

"Okay," she heard herself saying, without nearly enough fight. "Maybe just for one night."

Dear Reader,

Stress. I have to say, for the most part, I have been blessed with a fairly stress-free life. But the past few months have been an exception to that. Most of it was my own fault. Like many of the women I know, I was saying yes when I should have been saying no. Even though the projects I took on were all things I wanted to do, and enjoyed, I ended up with way too much on the go. I started feeling as if I did not have enough time or energy for anything. And then I had a couple of completely unexpected events thrown into the mix, things that were completely out of my control. I coped terribly. I became a quivering mass of anxiety.

Having said that, I *did* cope, and I did make it through. Love was waiting in unexpected places. Laughter lifted me up.

I know some of you reading this, right now, are in that very place. And so this is my invitation to you: *stop*. Settle in with this book and let it take your mind off your problems for a little while. Enjoy. Breathe. Relax. I hope there are some elements in this story that inspire you, that shed some light on your own strength, and I hope it gives you those healing moments of laughter that make it possible to go on.

With love and best wishes,

Cara Colter

The Pregnancy Secret

Cara Colter

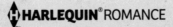

Recycling programs
for this product may
not exist in your area.

ISBN-13: 978-0-373-74336-0

The Pregnancy Secret

First North American Publication 2015

Copyright © 2015 by Cara Colter

This edition published by arrangement with Harlequin Books S.A.

For questions and comments about the quality of this book,
please contact us at CustomerService@Harlequin.com.

® and TM are trademarks of Harlequin Enterprises Limited or its
corporate affiliates. Trademarks indicated with ® are registered in the
United States Patent and Trademark Office, the Canadian Intellectual
Property Office and in other countries.

Printed in U.S.A.

Cara Colter shares her life in beautiful British Columbia, Canada, with her husband, nine horses and one small Pomeranian with a large attitude. She loves to hear from readers, and you can learn more about her and contact her through Facebook.

Books by Cara Colter

HARLEQUIN ROMANCE

The Cop, the Puppy and Me
Battle for the Soldier's Heart
How to Melt a Frozen Heart
Rescued by the Millionaire
The Millionaire's Homecoming
Interview with a Tycoon
Meet Me Under the Mistletoe

Mothers in a Million

Second Chance with the Rebel

The Gingerbread Girls

Snowflakes and Silver Linings

Visit the Author Profile page
at Harlequin.com for more titles.

To my friend, and mentor, Joan Fitzpatrick, whose wisdom and compassion have guided and inspired me for three decades.

CHAPTER ONE

A BLOCK AWAY from a destination he had no desire to reach, it pierced Kade Brennan's distracted mind that something was wrong.

Very wrong.

There were no sirens, but the strobes of the blue and red bar lights on top of half a dozen police cruisers were pulsing strenuously. It was jarringly at odds with the crystal clear morning light that filtered, a suffused lime green, through the unfurling spring leaves of the huge cottonwoods that lined the shores of the Bow River.

Now, above the sounds of a river bloated with spring runoff, above the sounds of the cheerful chirping of birds, above the sounds of the morning rush of traffic, Kade could hear the distinctive static of emergency frequency radios. A robotic female voice was calling a code he did not understand. It looked as if there was an ambulance in that cluster of emergency vehicles.

Kade broke into a run, dodging traffic as he cut across the early-morning crush of cars on Memorial Drive to the residential street on the other side.

It was one of those postcard-pretty Calgary blocks that looked as if nothing bad could ever happen on it. It was an older neighborhood of arts and crafts–style houses, many of them now turned into thriving cottage businesses. Nestled under the huge canopies of mature trees, Kade noted, were an art-supply store, an organic bakery, an antiques shop and a shoe store.

This neighborhood was made even more desirable by the fact it was connected to downtown Calgary by the Peace Bridge, a pedestrian-only walkway over the river that Kade had just crossed.

Except at this moment the postcard-pretty street that looked as if nothing bad could ever happen on it was completely choked with police cars. People walking to work had stopped and were milling about.

Kade, shouldering through them, caught bits of conversation.

"What happened?"

"No idea, but from the police presence, it must be bad."

"A murder, maybe?" The speaker could not hide the little treble of excitement at having his morning walk to work interrupted in such a thrilling fashion.

Kade shot him a dark look and shoved his way, with even more urgency, to the front of the milling crowd, scanning the addresses on the cottagey houses and businesses until he found the right one. He moved toward it.

"Sir?" A uniformed man was suddenly in front of him, blocking his path. "You can't go any farther."

Kade ignored him, and found a hand on his arm.

Kade shook off the hand impatiently. "I'm looking for my wife." Technically, that was true. For a little while longer anyway.

"Kade," Jessica had said last night over the phone, "we need to discuss the divorce." He hadn't seen her for more than a year. She'd given him the address on this street, and he'd walked over from his downtown condo, annoyed at what his reluctance about meeting her was saying about him.

All this was certainly way too complicated

to try to explain to the fresh-faced young policeman blocking his way.

"Her name is Jessica Brennan." Kade saw, immediately, in the young policeman's face that somehow all these police cars had something to do with her.

No, something in him screamed silently, a wolf howl of pure pain, *no*.

It was exactly the same silent scream he had stifled inside himself when he'd heard the word *divorce*. What did it mean, he'd asked himself as he hung up his phone, that she wanted the divorce finalized?

Last night, lying awake, Kade had convinced himself that it could only be good for both of them to move on.

But from his reaction to this, to the fact all these police cars had something to do with her, he knew the lie he had told himself—that he didn't care—was monstrous in proportion.

"She's okay, I think. There's been a break-in. I understand she was injured, but it's non-life-threatening."

Jessica injured in a break-in? Kade barely registered the non-life-threatening part. He felt a surge of helpless fury.

"She's okay," the young cop repeated. "Go that way."

It was upsetting to Kade that his momentary panic and rage had shown in his face, made him an open book to the cop, who had read his distress and tried to reassure.

He took a second to school himself so that he would not be as transparent to Jessica. He looked up the walk he was being directed to. Twin white lilacs in full and fragrant bloom guarded each side of a trellised gate. The house beyond the gate was the house Jessica had always wanted.

It was a cute character cottage, pale green, like the fresh colors of spring all around it. But it wasn't her home. A sign hung over the shadowed shelter of an inviting porch.

Baby Boomer, and in smaller letters, Your Place for All Things Baby.

Jessica had given him only the house number. She hadn't said a word about *that*.

And he knew exactly why. Because, for a moment, that familiar anger was there, over-riding even the knife of panic that had begun to ease when the young cop had said she was okay. *Hell's bells, did she never give up?*

Or was the anger because the house, her new business and that phone call last night were evidence that she was ready to move on?

It was not as if, Kade told himself sternly,

he wasn't ready to move on. In fact, he already had. He was just completely satisfied with the way things were. His company, Oilfield Supplies, had reached dizzying heights over the past year. Without the complication of a troubled relationship, he had been able to focus his attention intensely on business. The payoffs had been huge. He was a man who enjoyed success. Divorce did not fit with his picture of himself.

Divorce.

It was going to force him to face his own failure instead of ignore it. Or maybe not. Maybe these days you just signed a piece of paper and it was done. Over.

Could something like that ever be over? Not really. He knew that from trying to bury himself in work for the past year.

If it was over, why did he still wear his ring? He had talked himself into believing it was to protect himself from the interest of the many women he encountered. Not personally. He had no personal life. But professionally he met beautiful, sophisticated, *interested* women every day. He did not need those kinds of complications.

He was aware, suddenly, he did not want Jessica to see he was still wearing that ring that bound him to her, so he took it off and slipped it in his pocket.

Taking a deep, fortifying breath, a warrior needing the opponent—when had Jessica become the opponent?—not to know he had a single doubt or fear, Kade took the wide steps, freshly painted the color of rich dairy cream, two at a time.

In startling and violent contrast to the sweet charm of the house, the glass had been smashed out of the squares of paned glass in the door. The door hung open, the catch that should have held it closed dangling uselessly.

Inside that door Kade skidded to a halt, aware of glass crackling under his feet. His eyes adjusted to the dimness as he burst out of the bright morning light. He had entered into a world more terrifying to him than an inhabited bear den.

The space was terrifying because of what was in it. It was the world he and Jessica had tried so hard to have and could not. It was a world of softness and light and dreamy hopes.

The stacks of tiny baby things made other memories crowd around Kade, of crying, and arguing, and a desperate sense of having come up against something he could not make right. Ever.

He sucked in another warrior's breath. There

was a cluster of people across the room. He caught a glimpse of wheat-colored hair at the center of it and forced himself not to bolt over there.

He would not let her see what this—her injury, this building full of baby things—did to him.

Unfortunately, if he was not quite ready to see her, he had to take a moment to gather himself, and that forced him to look around.

The interior dividing walls within the house had been torn down to make one large room. What remained for walls were painted a shade of pale green one muted tone removed from that of the exterior of the house. The large space was connected by the expanse of old hardwood, rich with patina, and yet rugs and bookcases had been used to artfully divide the open area into four spaces.

Each was unique, and each so obviously represented a nursery.

One was a fantasy in pink: the crib was all done in pink flowered bedding, with pink-striped sheets and a fluffy pink elephant sprawled at the center. A polka-dot pink dress that looked like doll clothes was laid out on a change table. The letters g-i-r-l were suspended by invisible threads from the ceiling. A rocking chair, with pillows that matched the bedding, sat at right angles to the crib.

The next space was a composition in shades of pale blue. The crib and its bedding, again, were the main focus, but the eye was drawn to the vignette of boyish things that surrounded it. There were toy trains and tractors and trucks displayed on the shelves of a bookcase. Miniature overalls and an equally miniature ball cap hung on an antique coatrack beside it. A pair of impossibly small work boots hung from their laces off the same rack.

Next was one all done in lacy white, like a wedding dress, a basket on the floor overflowing with white stuffies: lambs and polar bears and little white dogs. The final display had two cribs, implying twins, and a shade of yellow as pale as baby duck down repeated in the bedding and lamp shades and teeny outfits.

Kade stood, sucking air into his chest, taking it all in and fighting the unmanly desire to cut and run.

How could Jessica do this? Work every day with the thing that had caused her, and him— and them—such unbelievable heartache? He felt all that anger with Jessica solidifying inside his chest. *Now* he was ready to face her.

He narrowed his eyes and looked to the clus-

ter of people. They were at the very back of
the old house, behind a counter with an old-
fashioned cash register perched on it. Feeling
as if his masculinity and size could damage the
spaces, he passed through them quickly, holding his breath and being careful not to touch
anything. Kade edged his way to the back of
the room, inserting a firmness into his step that
he did not feel.

It was unnecessary, because she didn't open
her eyes as Kade arrived at the back of the
store. Jessica was strapped to a wheeled gur-
ney. Her eyes were tightly shut. A uniformed
medic was leaning over her, splinting her right
arm below her shoved-up sleeve. Two police
officers, a man and a woman, stood by, note-
pads out.

Seeing Jessica would have been, at any time,
like taking a punch to the stomach. But seeing
her like this was unbearable.

It reminded him of the hardest lesson his
marriage had taught him: even though it was
his deepest desire, he had been unable to protect her.

Studying her now, without her awareness,
Kade could see subtle changes in her. She
looked oddly grown-up in a buttoned-up white
blouse and a gray pencil skirt. Her slender feet

were encased in a pair of very practical and very plain flat pumps. She looked professional, and yet oddly dowdy, like that British nanny on television. Her look, if it could be called that, filled him with a certain sense of relief.

Jessica was obviously not out to capture a man.

But she looked so serious, not that he expected her to be upbeat, given the circumstances. She looked every inch the pragmatic businesswoman she had evidently become, rather than the artist she had always been. He was pretty sure the only day he'd ever seen Jessica out of jeans was the day they'd gotten married.

Her hair was the same color, untouched by dye, wheat ripening in a field, but had been bobbed off short, in a way that made her features seem elegant and chiseled and mature rather than gamine and friendly and girlish. Or maybe it was because she had lost weight that her features, especially her cheekbones, seemed to be in such sharp relief. She had on not a drop of makeup. Again, Kade felt a completely unwanted niggle of relief. She was obviously not making the least effort to play up her natural beauty.

Despite the fact she looked both the same and

different, despite the fact she looked pale and bruised and despite the fact she was dressed in a way that suggested she did not like drawing attention to herself, Jessica did what she had always done, even though he tried to steel himself against reacting to her.

From the first moment he had seen her laughter-filled face on campus, he had been captivated. She had been sitting with friends at an outdoor picnic area. She had looked his way just as he was crossing a huge expanse of lawn, late for class.

His heart had done then exactly what it did now. It had stood still. And he had never made that class. Instead, he had crossed the lawn to her and to his destiny.

Jessica—then Clark—hadn't been beautiful in the traditional way. A little powder had not done anything to hide her freckles, which had already been darkening from the sun. Her glossy hair, sun streaked, had been spilling out of a clip at the back of her head. She'd been supercasual in a pink T-shirt and jean shorts with frayed cuffs. Her toenails had been painted to match her shirt.

But it was her eyes that had captivated him: as green as a leprechaun's and sparkling with just as much mischief. She had, if he recalled correctly, and he was sure he was, been wearing just a hint of makeup that day, shadow around her eyes that made them the deep, inviting green of a mountain pond. Her smile had been so compelling, warm, engaging, full of energy, infused with a force of life.

But two years of marriage had stripped her of all of that effervescent joy. And he could see, from the downturned line around her mouth, it had not returned. Kade welcomed the iciness he felt settle around his heart.

He had not been enough for her.

Still, even with that thought like an acid inside him, he could not stop himself from moving closer to her.

He was shocked that he wanted to kiss her forehead, to brush the hair back from the smoothness of her brow. Instead, he laid his palm over her slender forearm, so aware his hand could encircle it completely. He saw that she was no longer wearing her rings.

"Are you okay?" The hardness Kade inserted in his voice was deliberate. There was no sense anyone knowing the panic he had felt, just for a moment, when he had thought of a world without Jessica. Especially not Jessica herself.

Jessica's eyes flew open. They were huge and familiar pools of liquid green, surrounded by lashes so thick they looked as if they had been rolled in chocolate cake batter. She had always had the most gorgeous eyes, and even her understated look now could not hide that. Unbidden, he thought of Jessica's eyes fastened on him, as she had walked down the aisle toward him… He shook off the memory, annoyed with himself, annoyed by how quickly he had gone *there*.

Now her beautiful eyes had the shadows of sorrow mixed with their light. Still, for one unguarded moment, the look in her eyes when she saw it was him made Kade wish he was the man she had thought he was. For one unguarded moment, he wished he was a man who had an ounce of hope left in him.

CHAPTER TWO

WARINESS TOOK THE place of what had flared so briefly in Jessica's eyes when she had seen it was him, Kade. A guard equal to the one he knew to be in his own gaze went up in hers.

"What are you doing here?" Jessica asked him, her brow knit downward.

What was he doing here? She had asked him to come. "Did she hit her head?" Kade asked the ambulance attendant.

Jessica's frown deepened. "No, I did not hit my head."

"Possibly," the medic said.

"What are you doing here?" Jessica demanded again. It was a tone he remembered too well, the faintest anger hissing below the surface of her words, like a snake waiting to strike.

"You asked me to come," Kade reminded her. "To discuss—" He looked at the crowd around them, and could not bring himself to finish the sentence.

"Oh!" She looked contrite. "Now I remember. We were meeting to discuss…" Her voice drifted away, and then she sighed. "Sorry, Kade, I truly forgot you were coming." Apparently she hadn't lain awake last night contemplating the *d-i-v-o-r-c-e*.

"It's been a crazy morning," she said, as if it needed clarification.

"So I can see," he said. Jessica. Master of the understatement.

"Who are you?" the woman police officer asked.

"I'm her husband." Well, *technically*, he still was.

Kade was only inches from Jessica, but he was so aware that the small physical distance between them was nothing compared with the emotional one. It could not be crossed. That was what hissed right below the surface of her voice. There was a minefield of memory between them, and to try to negotiate it felt as if it would be risking having them both being blown to smithereens.

"I think her arm is fractured or broken," the medic said to Kade, and then returned his attention to Jessica. "We're going to transport you. They'll do X-rays at the hospital. I'm going to call ahead so they'll be ready for you in the emergency department."

"Which hospital?" Kade asked.

"You don't need to come," Jessica said, and there was *that* tone again, her apology apparently forgotten. She glared at Kade in warning when he frowned at her.

She was right. He did not *need* to go with her. And he could not have stopped himself if he tried.

"Nonetheless," he said, "I'd be more at ease making sure you were okay."

"No."

Kade knew that tone: she had made up her mind and there would be no getting her to change it.

No matter how stupidly unreasonable she was being.

"I thought he was your husband," the woman police officer said, confused.

"You don't need to come to the hospital," Jessica said. She tried to fold her arms over her chest. The splint on her right arm made it awkward enough that after three attempts she gave up. She glared at her arm accusingly, and when that brought her no relief, she switched her glare to him.

To what he could tell was her chagrin, he accomplished what she had not been able to. He folded his arms firmly over his chest.

Battle stations.

What did this mean that he was insisting on accompanying Jessica to the hospital? That he was accepting responsibility for her?

Had he ever stopped feeling responsible for her?

"I thought he was your husband," the police officer said again.

"I am," Kade said, and heard the same firmness in his voice as that day that felt as if it was so long ago when he had said, "I do."

Jessica felt a shiver travel up and down her spine.

Her husband.

She watched Kade standing there, so close she could smell the familiar heady scent of him, his arms folded firmly over the deepness of that chest. He looked grim and formidable when he took that stance.

And even with that intimidating scowl drawing his dark brows down and pulling the edges of his mouth? Kade was the most magnificently made man Jessica had ever encountered. And she was pretty sure the female police officer wasn't immune to that fact, either.

Jessica had never tired of looking at him, not even when their relationship had become so troubled. Sometimes it had made her anger even more complicated that she still liked to look at him when he was so aggravating!

But gazing at him now, she felt resignation. This morning Kade had on a beautifully cut summer suit that she was certain was custom made. With it he had on a plain white shirt, possibly Egyptian cotton, and a subdued, expertly knotted tie, the slight luster of it screaming both silk and expense.

The ensemble made him look every inch the president and CEO of one of Calgary's most successful companies. Despite a rather mundane name, Oilfield Supplies did just that. It supplied the frantic oilfield activity of Alberta and beyond. With Kade's work ethic, ambition and smarts, the company's rise, in the past few years, had been mercurial.

And yet there was nothing soft looking about the man. There was none of the slender build or office pallor of a desk worker about him. He had learned his business from the bottom up, working on rigs to put himself through university. Despite the beautiful clothing, that rugged toughness was still in the air around him. Kade Brennan, with those long legs and those broad shoulders, and that deep chest, radiated pure power.

He had mink-dark hair. It managed, somehow, to look faintly unruly, no matter how short he cut it. And right now, that was very short.

He was clean shaven—Jessica had never known him not to be—and the close shave showed off the masculine perfection of his face: great skin, high cheekbones, straight nose, full lips, faintly jutting chin.

And his damn eyes, sexy and smoldering, were the deep sapphire of the ocean water. It was a color she had seen replicated only once, off the southernmost tip of the Big Island of Hawaii, where they had gone for their honeymoon.

But well before she'd had that reference point, from practically the moment she had met him, Jessica had spent an inordinate amount of time dreaming what their baby would look like. Would it have his eyes or hers, or some incredible combination of both?

The knife edge of that familiar pain was worse than the pain that throbbed along the length of her arm, despite the ice packs splinted in with her limb that were supposed to be giving her relief from pain.

Her husband.

She could feel her heart begin a familiar and hard tattoo at all that had once meant, and at all she knew about this man, the delicious intimacies that only a wife could know.

That he had ticklish toes, and loved the smell of lemons, and that if you kissed that little groove behind his ear, he was putty—

Jessica made herself stop, annoyed that she had gone *there* so swiftly. With everything between them, how was it she could feel this when she saw him? As if she had made the slow, chugging climb up the roller coaster and was now poised at the very summit, waiting to plunge down?

With everything between them, it felt like a betrayal of herself that she could feel such a deep and abiding hunger for the familiar feeling of his arms around her, for the scrape of his cheek across her own, for his breath in her ear, for the gentle savagery of his lips claiming her lips and his body claiming her body.

Her husband.

She felt weak. Where was her newfound sense of herself when she needed it most? Where was her fledgling self-respect? Where was her feeling that her life was working, and that she could have dreams she had set aside when Kade had walked away from her?

Jessica had discovered she could be responsible for her own dreams. It was really much easier without the complications of a man! In fact, she had decided the things she was dreaming would be so much more attainable without a man, especially one like him, who was just a little too sure that he knew the right answers for everybody.

Jessica was certain Kade would not approve of the secret she held inside herself. It was a secret that gave her pure joy, just as once an ultrasound picture tucked in a pocket close to her heart had. She had made a decision to adopt a baby.

It was at the very initial stages, little more than a thought, but she wanted things between her and Kade finalized before she even started the application process. She reminded herself that she needed to be strong for this meeting with Kade, and she despised the unexpected weakness of desire.

She'd rehearsed for a week before she'd called him, striving for just the right all-business tone of voice, planning this morning's meeting so carefully…

Of course, being caught in the middle of a

breaking and entering had not been part of her plan! She could not believe, in all the chaos, she had totally forgotten he would be coming.

That was it. That explained the way she was feeling right now. She'd just had quite the shock. The pain in her arm was throbbing mercilessly, and despite denying it to the medic, it was possible she'd hit her head in the scuffle. Maybe, just maybe, a tiny bit of weakness in the department of her husband was acceptable.

Except right now she needed to be strong around him, not weak!

She stole another look at him. There was no missing how ill at ease the store made him. Something in his closed expression even suggested anger. At that realization, that he was angry, something in her hardened. She had known he might react like this when she'd invited him here.

And she had told herself firmly that it was a test she needed to pass. Divorcing Kade, not just on paper, but with her heart, would involve not caring what he liked or didn't like about her choices.

Her lawyer was absolutely right. It was time to tie up some loose ends in her life. And the lawyer was not even aware of *all* the reasons why it had become so important. Her lawyer knew only about her thriving business. Her decision to adopt was a secret, for now.

But it was a secret that required her to acknowledge that Kade Brennan, the husband she had been separated from for more than a year, was one gigantic loose end!

"What happened here?" Kade asked, but typical Kade, he wasn't asking. He was demanding, ready to take charge.

And she was never going to admit what a relief it would be to let him. "Really, Kade, it's none of your business."

The female officer, in particular, looked taken aback at her tone. "I thought he was your husband," she said again, almost plaintively.

"We're nearly divorced," Jessica explained, trying for the cavalier note of a career woman who didn't care, but she had to physically brace herself from flinching from the word.

Divorced.

She'd rehearsed that word, too, trying to take the bitter edge out of it, the sense of loss and finality and failure.

"Oh." If she was not mistaken, Officer—Jessica squinted at her name tag—Kelly took to that information like a starving hound scenting a bone.

"What happened here?" Kade asked again.

Jessica glared at him. To her relief, the medic announced they were ready to go, and she was wheeled out past Kade before having to give in to his demand for answers. Behind her, to her annoyance, she could hear the police officer filling him in on what had happened. She glanced back to see the female officer blinking helpfully at Kade and checking her notes.

"She came in to do paperwork this morning, six o'clock. Someone broke in around seven thirty."

"Don't come to the hospital," Jessica called over her shoulder, feeling a childish desire to get in the last shot. "I don't need you."

She glanced back one more time just as they crossed through her doorway to outside, where throngs of people seemed to be gathered in front of her house. But she didn't really even notice. What she noticed was that her arrow had hit home.

Kade looked momentarily stricken by her words.

That she didn't need him.

And instead of feeling happy that she had drawn blood, she felt sick about it, and some little demon inside her had to try to repair it, and let him know he was needed after all.

"Actually, Kade, can you find a way to secure everything? Please?"

Really, after her remark that she didn't need him, he should tell her to go get stuffed. But he didn't.

"And if you could put up a closed-for-the-day sign over that broken window I'd be most appreciative."

He snorted, but didn't say no.

"I can't just leave things. The door is broken. He could come back. Anybody could come in and just start helping themselves to everything in here."

All her hopes and dreams. It was a strange twist that she was being forced to ask Kade to rescue them.

"Never mind," Jessica said, appalled that she had even asked him. "I'll call someone."

She didn't need him. She didn't! Why was she giving him this mixed message: "I need you. I don't need you." She had the stunning realization she was not as clear of her soon-to-be ex-husband as she thought she was!

"I'll look after it," he said.

She should have protested harder, but there was no denying what a relief it was to have Kade Brennan, her husband for a little while longer, say that he would look after things.

CHAPTER THREE

JESSICA WAS WHEELED out to the ambulance, and Kade prowled through her shop looking for items to repair her door. Finally, in a back drawer in a tiny kitchen area he found a hammer and regarded it thoughtfully.

"This isn't really a hammer," he muttered to himself. "It's more like a toy, a prop for one of her fake nurseries."

In a dank cellar, he found some old boards. Thankfully, they had nails in them that he could pull and reuse. Why did women never have the essentials? Nails, screwdrivers, hammers, duct tape?

He boarded up the broken front door and found a square of thick wood to write a few words on.

He had to nail it up over the broken window because of the lack of duct tape. A determined thief could still get in, but the repair, though not pretty, actually looked quite a bit more secure than her old door with its paned glass.

He surveyed his work briefly, and recognized it as temporary but passable. Then he called his personal assistant, Patty, to tell her he would be very late today, if he made it in at all. "I need you to find me a simple surveillance system. I think there's a kind that alerts to your phone. And then could you find a handyman? I need a door fixed, a window replaced and that surveillance system installed. Have him call me for the details.

"And also if you could have my car dropped at Holy Cross Hospital? Whoever brings it can just give me a call when they get there, I'll meet them for keys." He listened for a moment. "No, everything is fine. No need for concern."

Kade walked out to Memorial Drive and was able to flag a cab to take him to the hospital.

He found Jessica in a wheelchair, in a waiting room in the X-ray department.

"How are you doing?"

It was obvious she was not doing well. Her face was pale, and she looked as if she was going to cry.

He could not handle Jessica crying. There was nothing he hated more than the helplessness that made him feel. To his detriment, he had not reacted well to her tears in the past.

He felt ashamed of the fact that she felt it necessary to suck in a deep, steadying breath before she spoke to him.

"They've done an X-ray. I'm just waiting for the doctor. It is broken. I'm not sure if they can set it, or if it will need surgery." She looked perilously close to tears.

Kade fought an urge to wrap his arms around her and let her cry. But he'd never been good with tears, and it felt way too late now to try to be a sensitive guy. It would require him to be a way better and braver man than he knew how to be.

She knew his weaknesses, because she set her shoulders and tilted her chin. "You didn't have to come."

He shrugged. "Your store is secure," he told her. "I put up a sign."

The struggle—whether to be gracious or belligerent—was evident in her eyes. Graciousness won, as he had known it would. "Thank you. What did it say?"

"Baby bummer, temporarily closed due to break-in."

A reluctant smile tickled her lips, and then she surrendered and laughed. "That's pretty good. Even though it's a major bummer, not a baby one."

Kade was pretty pleased with himself that he had made her laugh instead of cry.

"It could have been a much more major bummer than it was," he said sternly. "Tell me what happened."

Jessica couldn't help but shiver at the faintly dangerous note in Kade's voice. She could not be intimidated by it!

"Isn't it fairly obvious what happened?" she asked coolly. "I was doing some paperwork, and there was a break-in."

"But he came through the front door."

"So?"

"Is there a back door?" Kade asked. That something dangerous deepened in his tone.

"Well, yes, but we just surprised each other. Thankfully, I called 911 as soon as I heard the glass break."

"Don't you think you could have run out the back door and called 911 from safety?"

Jessica remembered what she didn't like about Kade. Besides everything. She needed a good cry right now and she was sucking it back rather than risk his disapproval. On top of that,

he was a big man at work. It made him think
he knew the answers to everything.

Which was why she didn't even want him to
know about adoption. He was certain to have
an opinion about that that she would not be
eager to hear.

"Hindsight is always twenty-twenty," she informed him snootily.

"How did you end up hurt?" Kade asked.

Jessica squirmed a bit.

"Um, we scuffled," she admitted. "I fell."

"You scuffled?" Kade asked, incredulous.
"You *scuffled* with a burglar? I would have
thought it was hard to scuffle while running
for the back door."

"I was not going to run away," she said.

"That is nothing to be proud of."

"Yes," she said, "it is. Don't you dare pre-
sume to tell me what to be proud of."

From their shared laughter over the bummers
of life just moments ago to this. It was just like
the final weeks of their marriage: arguments
lurked everywhere.

"Why are you proud of it?" he asked, that
dangerous something still deepening in his
tone, that muscle jerking along the line of his
jaw that meant he was *really* annoyed.

"I'm proud I took on that scrawny thief," Jessica said, her voice low, but gaining power. "I lost my mother when I was twelve. I've lost two babies to miscarriage."

And she had lost Kade, not that she was going to mention that. In some ways the loss of him had been the worst of all. The other losses had been irrevocable, but Kade was still there, just not there for her.

"Sorry?" he said, reeling back slightly from her as if she had hit him with something. "What does that have to do with this?"

"I am not losing anything else," she said, and could hear the tautness in her own voice. "Not one more thing."

He stared at her, and she took a deep breath and continued.

"You listen to me, Kade Brennan. I am not surrendering to life anymore. I am not going to be the hapless victim. I am making the rules, and I am making my own life happen."

Kade was shocked into silence, so she went on, her tone low. "So if that means scuffling with someone who was trying to take one more thing from me, then so be it."

"Oh, boy," he said, his voice low and pained. "That's not even sensible."

"I don't care what you think is sensible," she said with stubborn pride.

Though, she did plan to be more sensible soon. Naturally, there would be no more scuffling once she had adopted a baby. She would think things all the way through then. She would be the model of responsible behavior.

She hoped there were no questions about how one would handle a break-in on the adoption application.

"So you weren't running for the back door," he deduced, regaining himself. "Not even close."

"Nope." The new Jessica refused to be intimidated. She met his gaze with determination. She was not going to be cowed by Kade. She was not one of his employees. She was nearly not even his wife. In a little while, they would practically be strangers.

At the thought, a little unexpected grayness swirled inside her—she was willing to bet that was a result of her injury, a bit of shock—but she fought it off bravely.

"I was not letting him get away," Jessica said. "The police were coming."

For a moment he was stunned speechless again. He clenched that muscle in his jaw tighter. She remembered she hated that about him, too: the jaw clenching.

His voice rarely rose in anger, but that muscle, leaping along the hard line of his jaw, was a dead giveaway that he was *really* irritated about something.

"Are you telling me—" Kade's voice was low and dangerous "—that you not only scuffled with the burglar, but you tried to detain him?"

"He was a shrimp," Jessica said defiantly.

"In case you haven't looked in the mirror recently, so are you. And he could have had a knife! Or a gun!" So much for his voice rarely being raised in anger.

"I wasn't going to stand by and let him steal from me!" At the look on Kade's face, she backed down marginally. "Okay, so maybe I didn't think it all the way through." Something that was definitely going to have to change once she embraced motherhood.

"Maybe?"

She was not sure why she felt driven to defend herself, even when she knew Kade was right and she was wrong. Not just defend herself, but goad him a little bit.

"Break-ins started on this block a few nights ago. No one can sleep at night. We all go down there and check our businesses. That business is everything to me now. It's my whole life."

He heard the unspoken, she was sure. That the business had replaced him as her whole life.

The jaw muscle was rippling beneath the line of his skin. She watched it, fascinated despite herself. He was *really* angry.

"You've been going down there in the middle of the night to check your business?"

It didn't seem nearly as clever now with Kade glaring at her.

"Yes, I have," she said, refusing to back down. "And I'll probably do it again tonight, since he got away."

Well, actually, she probably wouldn't, but there was no sense Kade thinking he could order her around, could control her with even a hint of his disapproval. Those days were over.

"You are not going down there tonight," Kade said. "For God's sake, Jessica, haven't you ever heard of security cameras?"

"Of course I've thought of security cameras. And security companies. But the options are many and the selection is huge," she said. "I've been trying to figure out what is best for me and my budget. Not that that is any of your business. And you don't have any say in how I decide to handle it. None whatsoever. You and I only have one thing left to discuss. And that is our divorce."

And unbidden, the thought blasted through her that *that* was a major bummer.

And the doctor, a lovely young woman, chose that moment to come out, X-rays in hand, and say, "Mr. and Mrs. Brennan?"

Mr. and Mrs. Brennan. That should not fill her with longing! That should not make Jessica wonder if there would ever be another Mrs. Brennan taking her place.

It was over. Their brief marriage was over. They were getting divorced. Kade's life was no longer any of her business, just as hers was no longer any of his.

She would probably change her name back to Clark. She could be Ms. Clark instead of Mrs. Brennan. The baby would be a Clark.

She wasn't thinking about a first name. She knew better than that. Or at least she should know better than that. A memory knifed through her: Kade and her poring over the baby-name books. Deciding on Lewis for a boy and Amelia for a girl.

And then the first miscarriage. And somehow, she could see now, in retrospect, what she had not seen then. From the moment Kade had asked her not to name that little lost baby, a crack had appeared between them.

No, she was determined to enjoy the success of her baby nursery design business and her new storefront as a means to an end. She could have it all.

She could fill her life with the thrill of obtaining those adorable outfits no other store would carry, those one-of-a-kind over-the-crib mobiles, those perfect lamb-soft cuddly teddy bears that everyone wanted and no one could find.

And someday, maybe sooner than later, the outfits would be for her own baby. She would design a nursery for her own baby.

"Don't," he'd whispered when she had started painting the walls of their spare room a pale shade of lavender the second time. "Please don't."

But now she didn't need his approval. She could do it all her way. She could finally, finally be happy. All the pieces were in place.

Weren't they? If they were, why did Jessica feel a sudden desire to weep? It was that crack on her head. It was the throbbing in her arm. It was her day gone so terribly wrong, nothing according to her plan.

"Mr. and Mrs. Brennan?" the doctor asked, again, baffled by the lack of response.

"Yes," Kade said.

"No," Jessica said at the very same time.

He looked stubborn, a look Jessica remembered well.

She didn't think she should admit a sudden urge to kill him in front of the doctor, so she shrugged. "We're nearly divorced," she informed the doctor. "He was just leaving."

Kade gave her a look, and then got to his feet and prowled around the small waiting area.

"Well, if you could come with me."

Jessica stood up from the wheelchair to follow the doctor. She wobbled. Kade was instantly at her side.

"Sit down," he snapped.

Really, she should not tolerate that tone of voice from him, that tendency to bossiness. But the sudden wooziness she felt left her with no choice.

Kade pushed her down the hallway with the doctor, and they entered a small examining room. The doctor put the X-rays up on a light board.

"It's not a complicated break," she said, showing them with the tip of her pen. "It's what we call a complete fracture. I'm going to set it and cast it. I think you'll be in the cast for about four weeks and then require some therapy after to get full mobility back."

Four weeks in a cast? But that barely registered. What registered was that this was her arm with the bone, showing white on the X-ray, clearly snapped in two. Her wooziness increased. She had to fight an urge to put her head between her knees.

"Is it going to hurt?" Jessica whispered, still not wanting Kade to see any sign of weakness from her.

"I wish I could tell you no, but even with the powerful painkiller I'm going to give you, yes, it's going to hurt. Do you want your husband to come with you?"

Yes, part of Jessica whimpered. But that was the part she had to fight! Aware of Kade's eyes on her, she tilted her chin. "No, I'm fine. Kade, you don't have to wait."

CHAPTER FOUR

YOU DON'T HAVE to wait was not quite as firm as *you can leave now.* Jessica forced herself not to look back at him as the doctor took her to a different room. But she had to admit she felt grateful that he did not appear to be leaving.

A half hour later, her arm in a cast and immobilized in a sling, with some prescription painkillers and some instructions in her other hand, Jessica was pushed by a nurse back to the waiting area. Her feeling of wooziness had increased tenfold.

Because she actually felt happy that Kade was still there. He sprang from a chair as soon as he saw her, and then shoved his hands into his pockets.

"You didn't have to wait," Jessica said in stubborn defiance of the relief.

"I'll make sure you get home safely," he said. "I had someone from the office drop off my car for me while I waited. I'll bring it around to that door over there."

And then, before she could protest on a number of fronts—that she didn't need him to drive her and that she was going back to work, not home—he was gone.

She didn't want to admit how good his take-charge attitude felt sometimes. By the time he'd arrived at the door, she'd realized there was no way she was going to work. She was also reluctant to concede how good it felt when he held open the door of his car for her and she slid from the wheelchair into its familiar luxury. Moments later, with the wheelchair returned, he put the car in gear and threaded through what was left of the morning rush with ease.

Why did she feel glad that he didn't have a different car? She shouldn't care at all. But he'd bought the car after they'd graduated from university, well before he'd been able to afford such a thing.

"But why?" she'd asked him when he had come and shown it to her. The high-priced car had seemed as if it should not be a priority to a recent university graduate.

"Because when I marry you, this is what we're driving away in."

And then he'd shown her the ring he couldn't

afford, either. Three months later, with the roof down and her veil blowing out the back, they had driven away to a shower of confetti and their cheering friends.

One of her favorite wedding pictures was of that scene, the car departing, a just-married sign tacked crookedly to the back bumper that trailed tin cans on strings. In that picture Kade had been grinning over his shoulder, a man who had everything. And she had been laughing, holding on to her veil to keep it from blowing off, looking like a woman embracing the wildest ride of her life.

Which marriage had definitely turned out to be, just not in the way she had expected. It had been a roller-coaster ride of reaching dizzying heights and plummeting into deep and shadowy valleys.

Jessica took a deep breath. She tried to clear her head of the memories, but she felt the painkilling drugs were impeding her sense of control. Actually, she did not know which impaired her judgment more: sitting in the car, so close to Kade, or the drugs.

She had always liked the way he drove, and though it felt like a weakness, she just gave herself over to enjoying it. The car, under his expert hand, was a living thing, darting smoothly in and out of traffic.

They pulled up in front of the house they had once shared. It was farther from downtown than her business, but still in a beautiful established southwest neighborhood with rows of single-story bungalows, circa 1950.

Oh, God, if getting in his car had nearly swamped her with memories, what was she going to do if he came into the house they had once shared? There was a reason she had asked him to meet her at her business.

"Kade," she said firmly, wrestling the car door open with her left arm, "we need to get a divorce."

Kade made himself turn and look at her, even though it was unexpectedly painful having her back in the passenger seat of the car.

He forced himself to really look at her. Beneath the pallor and the thinness, he suspected *something*.

"What aren't you telling me?"

She wouldn't look at him. She got the car door open, awkward as it was reaching across herself with her left arm.

"You could have waited for me to do that,"

he said, annoyed, but she threw him a proud glare, found her feet and stepped out.

But her fighting stance was short-lived. She got a confused look on her face. And then she went very white. And stumbled.

He bolted from the car and caught her just as her legs crumpled underneath her. He scooped her up easily and stared down at her. And there he was, in the predicament he would have least predicated for the day—with Jessica's slight weight in his arms, her body deliciously pliant against his, her eyes wide on his face. She had a scent that was all her own, faintly lemony, like a chiffon pie.

She licked her lips, and his eyes moved to them, and he remembered her taste, and the glory of kissing Jessica.

She seemed to sense the sudden hiss of energy between them and regained herself quickly, inserted her good hand between them and shoved. "Put me down!"

As if he had snatched her up against her will instead of rescuing her from a fall. He ignored her and carried her up the walkway to the house.

Their house.

He was not going to carry her across the threshold. The memory of that moment in their history was just too poignant. He set her down on the front steps and her legs folded. She sat down on the top stair, looking fragile and forlorn.

"I don't feel well and I don't know where my keys are," she said.

He still had one, but he wasn't sure if he should use it. It felt presumptuous. It didn't feel as if he should treat it like his house anymore.

"I must have left my purse at the shop," she said, trying to get up.

"Sit still for a minute," he said.

It wasn't an order, just a suggestion, but she folded her good arm over the one in the sling. He half expected she might stick her tongue out at him, but she didn't.

"You've lost weight," he said, watching her sit on the stoop.

"A little," she admitted, as if she was giving away a state secret. "You know me. Obsessed about my projects. Right now it's launching Baby Boomer. Sometimes I forget to eat."

He frowned at that. She was always obsessed about something. Once, it had been about him.

"What's your sudden panic to get a divorce?" he asked.

She choked and glared at him. "Over a year is not a sudden panic."

"Have you met someone?" His voice sounded oddly raw in his own ears.

Jessica searched his face but he kept his features cool.

"Not that it is any of your business, but no." She hesitated. "Have you?"

He snorted. "No, I'm cured, thanks."

"I am, too!" She hesitated again, not, he guessed, wanting to appear too interested in his life. "I suppose you're playing the field, then?"

"What? What does that mean, exactly?"

"Seeing lots of women."

He snorted and allowed himself to feel the insult of it. Jessica was painting him as a playboy? "You have to know me better than that."

"You live in that building. It has a reputation."

"The condominium has a reputation?" he asked, astounded. "The building I live in? River's Edge?"

"It does," she said firmly. "Lots of single people live there. Very wealthy single people. It has a pool and that superswanky penthouse party room. The apartments are posh."

"How do you know all that?" he asked.

She turned red. "Don't get the idea I've been sneaking around spying on you."

"That is the furthest from any idea I would ever get about you," he said drily.

"The newspaper did a feature on it."

"I must have missed that."

"It seems like a good place for a single guy to live. One who is, you know, in pursuit of fun and freedom."

That was what Jessica thought he was in pursuit of? Jeez. Well, let her think it. How could it be that she didn't know him at all?

"Rest assured—" he could hear the stiffness in his voice "—I live there because it is a stone's throw from work, which by the way is where I spend the majority of my waking hours." He hesitated, not wanting to appear too interested in her life, either. "So are *you* playing the field?"

"Don't be ridiculous," she said.

"How come it's ridiculous when I ask but not when you ask?" And there it was, the tension between them, always waiting to be fanned to life.

"I already told you I'm obsessed with my business. I don't have time for anything else."

"So you are not in a new relationship, and apparently not looking for one. You want a divorce why?"

She sighed with what he felt was unnecessary drama. "We can't just go on indefinitely like this, Kade."

He wanted to ask why not but he didn't.

"All those hours I spend working are paying off. My business is moving to the next level."

He raised an eyebrow at her.

"I did over a hundred thousand in internet sales last year."

He let out a low appreciative whistle. "That's good."

"I think it could be double that this year with the storefront opening."

So she was moving up as well as on. Well, good for her. No sense admitting, not even to himself, how happy he was that her moving on did not involve a new guy moving in.

"My lawyer has advised me to tie up any loose ends."

He managed, barely, not to wince at being referred to as a loose end. "So your lawyer is afraid of what? That you'll be wildly success-ful and I, as your legal partner, will come in and demand half your business?"

"I suppose stranger things have happened," she said coolly.

"I think my business is probably worth as much as your business if we were going to start making claims against each other."

"We both know your business is probably worth a hundred times what my little place is worth. It's not about that."

"What's it about, then?" He was watching her narrowly. He knew her so well. And he knew there was something she wasn't telling him.

She sighed heavily. "Kade, we don't even have a separation agreement. We own this house together. And everything in it. You haven't even taken a piece of furniture. We need to figure things out."

He rolled his shoulders and looked at *their* house, the hopeless little fixer-upper that she had fallen in love with from the first moment she had laid her eyes on it.

"It's like the cottage in *Snow White*," she had said dreamily.

It hadn't been anything like the cottage in *Snow White*. Except for the decorative shutters, with hearts cut out of them, the house had been an uninspired square box with ugly stucco. The only thing Snow Whitish about it? It needed seven dwarfs, full-time, to help with its constant need for repair.

She had not done one thing to the exterior since he had left. They hadn't been able to afford too much at the time, so they had rented one of those spray-painter things and redone the stucco white. The black shutters and door had become pale blue.

"Isn't the color a little, er, babyish?" he had asked her of the pale blue.

Her sigh of pure delight, as if the color was inviting a baby into their house, seemed now, in retrospect, as if it might have been a warning.

Their strictly cosmetic changes were already deteriorating.

Was it the same inside as it had been? Suddenly he felt driven to know just how much she had moved on. It felt as if he needed to know.

He looked on his chain and acted surprised. "I have a key."

And a moment later he was helping her into the home they had shared. He had thought she would, if sensible, rip out every reminder of him.

But she was the woman who had scuffled with a burglar, and she had not done the sensible thing.

Their house was relatively unchanged. He thought she might have tried to erase signs of him—and them—but no, there was the couch they had picked out together, and the old scarred wooden bench she had fallen in love with and used as a coffee table. She hadn't even gotten rid of the oversize fake leather burgundy recliner with the handy remote control holder built into it. He had thought it would go. When people had come over she had referred to it, apologetically, as the guy chair, her nose wrinkled up with affectionate resignation. She had even named it Behemoth.

In fact, as far as Kade could see, the only change was that the bench contained only a mason glass jar spilling purple tulips. It was not covered with baby magazines. Oh. And there was one other thing changed. Their wedding pictures, her favorite shots in different-size frames, were not hung over the mantel of the fireplace. The paint had not faded where they had hung, and so there were six empty squares where once their love for each other had been on proud display.

The fireplace didn't actually work. He remembered their excitement the first time they had tried to light it, the year's first snow falling outside. The chimney had belched so much black smoke back into the house they had run outside, choking on soot and laughter. There was still a big black mark on the front of it from that.

He led her through the familiar space of the tiny house to the back, where the kitchen was. One day, they had hoped to knock out a wall and have open concept, but it had not happened. He made her sit at the table, another piece of furniture they had bought together at the secondhand stores they had loved to haunt on Saturday mornings. Without asking her, he fetched her a glass of water, finding the glasses with easy familiarity.

He remembered trying to paint the oak cabinets white in an effort to modernize the look of the kitchen. It had been disastrous. They had fallen asleep tucked against each other, propped against a cupboard, exhausted, covered in more paint than the cabinets. The cabinets looked as awful as they always had, the old stain bleeding through the white. They'd never bothered to try painting them again. The truth was, he liked them like that, with their laughter and ineptitude caught for all time in the hardened paint dribbles. And he thought she probably did, too.

The memories all felt like a knife between his eyes.

CHAPTER FIVE

BUT OF COURSE, Kade knew, those happy memories of renovation disaster had all happened before everything went south. After Jessica had discovered she was pregnant the first time, renovation had slammed to a halt.

Chemicals. Dust. The possibility of stirring up mouse poo.

Jessica took a sip of the water, watching him over the rim. "We need to make a decision about the house."

"You can have it," he said. "I don't want it."

"I don't want you to give me a house, Kade," she said with irritating patience, as if she was explaining the multiplication tables to a third grader. "I actually don't want this house. I'd like to get my half out of it and move on."

She didn't want the house with the fireplace that didn't work and laughter captured in the paint dribbles? She'd always loved this house, despite its many flaws.

There was something more going on that she was not telling him. He always knew. She was terrible at keeping secrets.

"I'll just sign over my half to you," he repeated.

"I don't want you to give it to me." Now she sounded mad. This was what their last weeks and months together had been like. There was always a minefield to be crossed between them. No matter what you said, it was wrong; the seeds were there for a bitter battle.

"That's ridiculous. Who says no to being given a house?"

"Okay, then. I'll give it to you."

"Why are you being so difficult?"

He could not believe the words had come out of his mouth. Their favorite line from *Beauty and the Beast*. In the early days, one of them had always broken the fury of an argument by using it.

For a moment, something suspiciously like tears shone behind her eyes, but then the moment was gone, and her mouth was pressed together in that stubborn "there is no talking to her now" expression.

"Can't we even get divorced normally?" she asked a little wearily, sinking back in her chair and closing her eyes.

"What does that mean?" he asked, but was sorry the minute the words were out of his mouth.

Of course, what it meant was that they hadn't been able to make a baby *normally*.

But thankfully, Jessica did not go there. "Normal—we're supposed to fight over the assets, not be trying to give them to each other."

"Oh, forgive me," he said sarcastically. "I haven't read the rule book on divorce. This is my first one."

Then he realized she was way too pale, and that she wasn't up for this. "You're not feeling very good, are you?"

"No," she admitted.

"We need to talk about this another time."

"Why do you always get to decide what *we* need?"

That stung, but he wasn't going to get drawn into an argument. "Look, you've had a tough morning, and you are currently under the influence of some pretty potent painkillers."

She sighed.

"You should probably avoid major decisions for forty-eight hours."

"I'm perfectly capable of making some decisions."

"There is ample evidence you aren't thinking right. You've just refused the offer of a house."

"Because I am not going to be your charity case! I have my pride, Kade. We'll sell it. You take half. I take half."

He shrugged, and glanced around. "Have you done any of the repairs that needed doing?"

Her mutinous expression said more than she wanted it to.

"Nothing is fixed," he guessed softly. "You're still jiggling the toilet handle and putting a bucket under the leak in the spare bedroom ceiling. You're still getting slivers in your feet from the floor you refuse to rip out, even though it was going to cost more to refurbish it than it would to put in a new one."

"That's precisely why I need to sell it," she said reasonably. "It's not a suitable house for a woman on her own."

Again, he heard something Jessica was not telling him.

"We'll talk about selling the house," he promised. "We'll probably get more for it if we do some fixes."

He noted his easy use of the word *we*, and backtracked rapidly. "How about if I come back later in the week? I'll have a quick look through the house and make a list of what absolutely has to be done, and then I'll hire a handyman to do it. My assistant is actually tracking one down to fix the door on your shop, so we'll see how he does there."

"I think the real estate agent can do the list of what needs to be done."

She'd already talked to a real estate agent. He shrugged as if he didn't feel smacked up the side of the head by her determination to rid herself of this reminder of all things *them*.

"Your real estate agent wants to make money off you. He is not necessarily a good choice as an adviser."

"And you are?"

He deserved that, he supposed.

"Okay. Do it your way," Jessica said. "I'll pay half for the handyman. Do you think you could come in fairly quickly and make your list? Maybe tomorrow while I'm at work?"

He didn't tell her he doubted she would be going back to work tomorrow. Her face was pale with exhaustion and she was slumped in her chair. No matter what she said, now was not the time for this discussion.

"I'm going to put you to bed," Kade said. "You're obviously done for today. We can talk about the house later." He noticed he carefully avoided the word *divorce*.

"I am exhausted," she admitted. "I do need to go to bed. However, you are not putting me to bed." She folded her one arm up over her sling, but winced at the unexpected hardness of the cast hitting her in the chest.

"I doubt if you can even get your clothes off on your own."

She contemplated that, looked down at her arm in the sling. He knew at that moment, the reality of the next four weeks was sinking in. In her mind, she was trying to think how she was going to accomplish the simple task of getting her clothes off and getting into pajamas.

"I'll go to bed in my clothes," she announced.

"Eventually," he pointed out, "you're going to have to figure out how to get out of them. You're going to be in that cast for how long?"

"A month," she said, horror in her features as her new reality dawned on her.

"I'll just help you this first time."

"You are not helping me get undressed," she said, shocked.

He felt a little shock himself at the picture in his mind of that very shirt sliding off the slenderness of her shoulders. He blinked at the old stirring of pure fire he felt for Jessica. She was disabled, for God's sake.

It took enormous strength to wrestle down the yearning the thought of touching her created in him, to force his voice to be patient and practical.

"Okay," Kade said slowly, "so you don't want me to help you get undressed, even though I've done it dozens of times before. What do you propose?"

Her face turned fiery with her blush. She glared at him, but then stared at her sleeve, bunched up above the cast, and the reality of trying to get the shirt off over the rather major obstacle of her cast-encased arm seemed to settle in.

"Am I going to have to cut it off? But I love this blouse!" She launched to her feet. He was sure it was as much to turn her back to him as anything else. She went to the kitchen drawer where they had always kept the scissors and yanked it open. "Maybe if I cut it along the seam," she muttered.

He watched her juggle the scissors for a minute before taking pity on her. He went and took the scissors away and stepped in front of her. Gently, he took her arm from the sling, and straightened the sleeve of the blouse as much as he could.

There was less resistance than he expected. Carefully, so aware of her nearness and her scent, and the silky feel of her skin beneath his fingertips, he took the sharp point of the scissors and slit the seam of the sleeve.

She stared down at her slit-open sleeve. "Thanks. I'll take it from here."

"Really? How are you going to undo your buttons?"

With a mulish expression on her face, she reached up with her left hand and tried to clumsily shove the button through a very tight buttonhole.

"Here," he said. "I'll help you."

She realized she could not refuse. "Okay," she said with ill grace. "But don't look."

Don't look? Hell's bells, Jessica, we belong to each other. Instead of getting impatient, he teased her. "Okay. Have it your way." He closed his eyes and placed his hand lightly on her open neckline. He loved the feel of her delicate skin beneath his fingertips. Loved it.

"What are you doing?" she squeaked.

"Well, if I can't look, I'll just feel my way to those buttons. I'll braille you. Pretend I'm blind." He slid his hand down. He felt her stop breathing. He waited for her to tell him to stop, but she didn't.

It seemed like a full minute passed before Jessica came to her senses and slapped his hand away.

He opened his eyes, and she was looking at him, her eyes wide and gorgeous. She licked her lips and his gaze went to them. He wanted to crush them under his own. That old feeling sizzled in the air between them, the way it had been before her quest for a baby had begun.

"Keep your eyes open," she demanded.

"Ah, Jessica," he said, reaching for her buttons, "don't look, but keep my eyes open. Is that even possible?"

"Try your best," she whispered.

"You are a hard woman to please." But, he remembered, his mouth going dry, she had not been a hard woman to please at all. With this memory of how it was to be together, red-hot between them, his fingers on her buttons was a dangerous thing, indeed.

Kade found his fingers on the buttons of her shirt. She stopped breathing. He stopped breathing.

Oh, my God, Jessica, he thought.

He did manage to keep his eyes open and not look. Because he held her gaze the whole time that he undid her buttons for her. His world became as it had once been: her. His whole world was suddenly, beautifully, only about the way the light looked in her hair, and the scent of her, and the amazing mountain-pond green of her eyes.

His hands slowed on her buttons as he deliberately dragged out the moment. And then he flicked open the last button and stepped back from her.

"There," he said. His voice had a raspy edge to it.

She stood, still as a doe frozen in headlights. Her shirt gapped open.

"You want me to help you get it off?"

She unfroze and her eyes skittered away from his and from the intensity that had leaped up so suddenly between them.

"No. No! I can take it from here."

Thank God, he thought. But he could already see the impracticality of it. "I'm afraid you'll fall over and break your other arm struggling out of those clothes," he told her. "The blouse is just one obstacle. Then there's, um, your tights."

"I can manage, I'm sure." Her tone was strangled. Was she imagining him kneeling in front of her, his hands on the waistband of those tights?

He took a devilish delight in her discomfort even while he had to endure his own.

"And I'm not sure what kind of a magician you would have to be to get your bra off with your left hand," he said.

She looked stricken as she went over the necessary steps in her mind.

"If you let me help you this time…" Kade suggested, but she didn't let him finish.

"No!"

"Okay." He put his hands in the air—cowboy surrender. And suddenly it didn't seem funny anymore to torment her. It just reminded him of all they'd lost. The easy familiarity between them was gone. The beautiful tension. The joy they had taken in discovering each other's bodies and the secrets of pleasing each other. In those first early days, he remembered chasing her around this little house until they were both screaming with laughter.

She blushed, and it seemed to him each of those losses was written in the contrived pride of her posture, too. Jessica headed for the hallway, the bedroom they had shared.

If he followed her there, there was probably no predicting what would happen next.

And yet he had to fight down the urge to trail after her.

What was wrong with him? What could happen next? She was on drugs. Her arm was disabled. She was being deliberately dowdy.

The simple truth? None of that mattered, least of all the dowdy part. Around Jessica, had he ever been able to think straight? Ever?

"While you're in there," he called after her, trying to convince her, or maybe himself, that he was just a practical, helpful guy, and not totally besotted with this woman who was not going to be his wife much longer, "you can pick what you're going to wear for the next four weeks very carefully."

"And while you're out there, you can start making a list of the fixes. Then you won't have to come back later."

To help her. He would not have to come back later to help her. He mulled that over. "I'm not sure how you can do this on your own. Think about putting on tights one-handed. It would probably be even more challenging than getting them off."

"I can go bare legged," she called.

"I don't even want to think about how you'll get the bra on," he said gruffly. He couldn't imagine how she was going to struggle into and out of her clothes, but that was not a good thing for him to be imagining anyway.

CHAPTER SIX

Jessica bolted through her bedroom and into the safety of her bathroom. She did not want Kade thinking about her bra, either!

But the reality of her situation was now hitting home.

Oh, there were practical realities. How was she going to manage all this? Not just dressing, which was going to be an inconvenience and a major challenge, but everything? How was she going to take a shower, and unpack boxes at Baby Boomer? How was she going to butter toast, for heaven's sake?

But all those practical realities were taking a backseat to the reality of how she had felt just now with Kade's hand, his touch warm and strong and beautiful, on her neck, and then on her buttons.

That was just chemistry, she warned herself. They had always had chemistry in abundance.

Well, not always. The chemistry had been challenged when they—no, she—had wanted it to respond on cue.

Still, it was easier to feel as if she could control the unexpected reality of Kade being in her home—their home—while she was comfortably locked in her bathroom.

Just to prove her control, she locked the door. But as she heard the lock click, she was very aware that she could not lock out the danger she felt. It was inside herself. How did you lock that away?

"Focus," Jessica commanded herself. But life seemed suddenly very complicated, and she felt exhausted by the complications. She wanted out of her clothes and into her bed.

She wanted her husband out of her house and she wanted the stirring of something that had slept for so long within her to go back to sleep!

Even if it did make her feel alive in a way she had not felt alive in a long, long time. Not even the excitement and success of her business had made her feel like this, tingling with a primal awareness of what it was to be alive.

Even the most exciting thing in her life—contemplating adopting a baby, and starting a family of her own—had never made her feel like this!

"That's a good thing," she told herself, out loud. "*This* feeling is a drug, a powerful, potent, addicting drug that could wreck everything."

But what a beautiful way to have it wrecked, a horrible uncontrollable little voice deep inside her whined.

"Everything okay in there?"

"Yes, fine, thanks." No, it wasn't fine. *Go away. I can't think clearly with you here.*

"I thought I heard you mumbling. Are you sure you're okay?"

"I'm fine," she called. She could hear a desperate edge in her own voice. Jessica was breathing hard, as if she had run a marathon.

Annoyed with herself, she told herself to just focus on one thing at a time. That one thing right now was removing her blouse. By herself.

Her nightie was hanging on the back of the bathroom door. She should not feel regret that the nightwear was mundane and not the least sexy. She should only be feeling thankful that it was sleeveless.

For a whole year, she had not cared what her sleepwear looked like. As long as it was comfortable she hadn't cared if it was frumpy, if it had all the sex appeal of a twenty-pound potato sack.

For a whole year, she had told herself that not

caring what she slept in, that not spending monstrous amounts of money on gorgeous lingerie, was a form of freedom. She had convinced herself it was one of the perks of the single life.

"Focus on getting your blouse off!" she told herself.

"Jessica?"

"I'm okay." She hoped he would not hear the edge in her voice. Of course, he did.

"You don't sound okay. I told you it was going to be more difficult than you thought."

What? Getting dressed? Or getting divorced?

One of the things that was so annoying about Kade? He had an aggravating tendency to be right.

"Focus," Jessica commanded herself. She managed to shrug the blouse off both her shoulders, and peeled the sleeve off her left arm with her teeth. But when she tried to slide the newly slit sleeve over the cast, it bunched up around it, and refused to move.

By now, Jessica was thoroughly sick of both Kade's tendency to be right and the blouse. It wasn't one of her favorites anymore. How was she going to ever wear it again without imagining his hands on the buttons?

She tugged at it. Hard. It made a ripping

sound. She liked that sound. She tugged at it harder.

"Argh!" She had managed to hurt her arm.

"Okay in there?"

"Stop asking!"

"Okay. There's no need to get pissy about it!"

She didn't want him telling her what to get pissy about! That was why she needed to divorce him.

She investigated the blouse. It was bunched up on the cast, and she had tugged at it so hard it was stuck there. She was afraid she was going to hurt her arm again trying to force it back off. Gentle prying was ineffectual. It refused to budge. The shoulder was too narrow to come down over the cast, and the fabric had ripped to the seams, but the seams held fast.

"That will teach me to buy such good quality," Jessica muttered, then waited for him to comment. Silence. One-handed, she opened every drawer in the bathroom looking for scissors. Naturally, there were none.

She would just have to forge ahead. So with the blouse hanging off her one arm increasing her handicap substantially, and by twisting herself into pretzel-like configurations, she managed to get the tights off. And then the skirt. She was sweating profusely.

Once the bra was off, she thought, it would be fairly simple to maneuver the nightgown over her head.

She reached behind her with her left hand and the bra gave way with delightful ease. She stepped out of it and let it fall in the heap with her tights and skirt.

The nightgown should be simple. If she left it hanging up as it was on the back of the bathroom door, she could just stick her head up under it, and it would practically put itself on. She grunted with satisfaction as she managed to get inside her nightie, put her left hand through the armhole and release it from its peg.

The nightie settled around her like a burka, her head covered, her face out the neck hole. That was okay. This angle should be good for getting her right arm up through the right armhole.

She tried to get her casted arm up. The nightie shifted up over her head as she found the right armhole and shoved. Of course, the blouse bunched around the cast prevented it from clearing the hole. It snagged on something.

So she was stuck with her arms in the air, and her head inside her nightgown.

She wiggled. Both arms. And her hips. Nothing happened.

With her left hand, she tried to adjust the nightie. She tugged down the neckline. Now half her head was out, one eye free. She turned to the mirror and peered at herself with her one uncovered eye. Her nightgown was hopelessly caught in her blouse, and her arm was stuck over her head.

And it hurt like the blazes.

She plunked herself down on the toilet seat and wriggled this way and that. She was sweating again.

There was a knock at the door.

She went very still.

"I made that list."

"Good," she croaked.

"Nothing on it I didn't expect. What do you think about the floors?"

She could not think about floors right now! She grunted as she tried again to free herself from her nightgown.

"Everything okay in there, Jessica?"

"I told you to stop asking!"

"I heard a thumping noise. You didn't fall, did you?"

"No."

"Are you okay?"

"Um—"

"It's a yes-or-no answer."

"Okay, then," she snapped with ill grace. "No." She unlocked the door.

He opened it. He stood there regarding her for a moment. She regarded him back, with her one eye that was uncovered, trying for dignity, her nightie stuck on her head, and her arm stuck in the air. "Don't you dare laugh," she warned him.

He snickered.

"I'm warning you."

"You are warning me what?" he challenged her.

"Not to laugh. And don't come one step closer."

Naturally, he ignored her on both fronts. Naturally, she was relieved, about him coming over anyway. Her arm was starting to ache unbearably. The smile on his lips she could have lived without.

Because there was really nothing quite as glorious as Kade smiling. He was beautiful at the best of times, but when that smile touched his lips and put the sparkle of sunshine on the sapphire surface of his eyes, he was irresistible.

Except she had to resist!

But then the smile was gone. Kade was towering over her. It occurred to her, from the draft she felt and the sudden scorching heat of his eyes, that the nightie was riding up fairly high on her legs.

Wordlessly, the smile gone, his expression all intense focus, he reached for where the blouse was stuck in the right-hand armhole of her nightgown. He began to unwind it. It gave easily to the ministrations of his fingers.

She said nothing.

"You see," he said softly, "there's nothing you can threaten me with that will work. Because the worst has already happened to me."

"What's that?" she demanded. How could he say the worst had happened to him when she was the one sitting here, humiliatingly trapped by her own clothing?

"You're divorcing me," he said softly. And then his face hardened and he looked as if he wanted to choke back the words already spoken.

CHAPTER SEVEN

THE NIGHTGOWN BROKE FREE, and her casted arm went through the right hole and the rest of the garment whispered around her. She used her left hand to tug the hem down to a decent level over her legs.

He bent his head and put his teeth on the fabric of her blouse, and the stubborn seam released. With one final, gentle tug that did not hurt Jessica's arm at all, the blouse was free from the cast.

"A good tailor can probably fix that," he said, laying the destroyed blouse in her lap.

"I'm not divorcing you," she said. "We're divorcing each other. Isn't that what you want?"

He found where her sling was discarded on the floor and looped it gently over her head.

"It seems to be what you want all of a sudden," he said. "There's something you aren't telling me, isn't there?"

She felt suddenly weak, as if she could blurt

out her deepest secret to him. How would it feel to tell him? *Kade, there is going to be a baby after all.*

No, that was not the type of thing to blurt out. What would be her motivation? Did she think it would change things between them? She didn't want them to change because of a baby. She wanted them to change because he loved her.

What? She didn't want things to change between them at all. She was taking steps to close this door, not reopen it! She was happy.

"Happy, happy, happy," she muttered out loud.

"Huh?"

"Oh. Just thinking out loud."

He looked baffled, as well he should!

"Go to bed," he told her. "We'll talk later. Now is obviously not the time."

He had that right! Where were these horrible, weak thoughts coming from? She needed to get her defenses back up.

With what seemed to be exquisite tenderness, he slipped her cast back inside the sling, adjusted the knot on the back of her neck.

His touch made her feel hungry for him and miss him more than it seemed possible. He put his hand on her left elbow and helped her up, and then across the bathroom and into the bedroom.

He let go of her only long enough to turn back the bedsheets and help her slide into the bed. She suddenly felt so exhausted that even the hunger she felt for her husband's love felt like a distant pang.

He tucked the covers up around her, and stood looking down at her.

"Okay," she said. "I'm fine. You can leave."

He started to go, but then he turned back and stood in the bedroom door, one big shoulder braced against the frame. He looked at her long and hard, until the ache came back so strong she had to clamp her teeth together to keep herself from flicking open the covers, an invitation.

Just like that, the intimacies of this bedroom revisited her. His scent, and the feel of his hands on her heated skin, his lips exploring every inch of her.

"Are you okay?" he asked. "You're beet red."

Flushed with remembered passion, how embarrassing.

She would do well to remember all that passion had not been able to carry them through heartbreak and turbulence.

She had bled all the passion out of this bedroom. She had become, she knew, obsessed with having a baby after the two miscarriages. It had become so horrible. Taking temperatures and keeping charts, and their lovemaking always faintly soured with her desperation.

Seeing him standing in the doorway, she remembered she had stood in that very spot watching him pack his things after their final night together.

"Please don't," she'd whispered.

"I can't stay."

"But why?"

Those cruel words that were forever a part of her now.

"Jessica, you've taken all the fun out of it."

"Out of making love?" she had asked him, stricken.

"Out of everything."

These were the things she needed to remember when a weak part of her yearned, with an almost physical ache, to be loved by him. To be held by him. To taste his lips again, and to taste faint salt on his skin after they'd made love. To feel the glory of his well-defined muscles under her fingertips. To smell him fresh out of the shower, to laugh with him until she could barely breathe for the ecstatic joy of it.

No, she needed to remember the pain, not

the glory, the loneliness and the disappointment, and all the hurtful things. She needed to remember when she had needed him—when she had felt so fragile it had seemed as if a feather falling on her could have cracked her wide-open—Kade had been unavailable in every way.

"I'm fine," she said to Kade now. "Please go."

He heard the coolness in her tone and looked offended by it, but she told herself she didn't care. She told herself she felt nothing but relief as she heard him close the door of the house behind him, and then lock the dead bolt with his key.

She told herself she didn't care that he had gone and that she was alone again. For a woman who was happy, happy, happy, she felt an overwhelming need to cry. With her good arm she grabbed her pillow and put it over her face to try to stifle her desire.

Desire. Why had that unfortunate word popped into her head? This further evidence of her weakness made her fight harder not to cry.

It was weak—it was not the woman she wanted to be. Today hardly even rated as a bad day. She'd had two miscarriages. *Those* had been bad days. She'd had the husband she loved madly leave her. *That* had been a bad day.

But despite her every effort to talk herself out of them, the tears came, and they came hard, and they came for every bad day Jessica had ever had.

Kade left the house and stood on the front step for a moment. There was a little peekaboo view of the downtown skyline. It was the only place on the property that had any kind of a view, and he and Jessica used to sit out here with a glass of wine on a summer's night, planning the deck they would build someday to capitalize on their sliver of a view.

But that had been before the pregnancy quest. Then wine, along with renovations, had been off her list.

He didn't want to go there.

He glanced at his watch and was shocked how early it was in the day. It wasn't even noon yet. It felt as if he had put in a full day, and a hard day, too. Still, there was a place he could go when he didn't want to go *there* for that walk down memory lane.

Work.

He called his assistant. The handyman had already been dispensed to Jessica's business. If he went and liked the guy's work, he could surrender the list. It might minimize encounters like the one he had just had.

He decided he liked the handyman, Jake, and he liked his work. Patty had provided him with the surveillance and security system she had found, and it was already installed when Kade arrived.

"It's really cool," Jake said. "It's motion activated, but you can program it to only send an image to your phone if a door or window is touched. Give me your phone number."

Kade had the fleeting thought it should be Jessica's number that he gave him, but on the other hand, how could he trust her not to rush right down here if her phone alerted her to an intruder?

He gave him his number, and they chortled like old friends as they experimented with setting the alarm and then touching the door, watching their images come up on Kade's phone. Along with the alarm system, a new door was nearly installed, and Jake had matched the old one very closely and even gotten one with shatterproof glass. He was reinforcing the frame so that the dead bolt would not break away.

But somehow when Kade left, the list for the fixes at the house he and Jessica shared was still in his pocket. He had not surrendered it to the obviously very capable handyman.

Why? He suspected it was not because he had not got an answer from her about the floors.

He mulled it over as he drove into the office. Somewhere between her house and there, he had decided he was doing the fixes himself.

But why?

He wasn't particularly handy. The state of the kitchen cupboards over there and the fireplace that did not work were ample evidence of that.

Then he knew. It was time to finish it. Not just the house, but all that house represented. It was time to finish his relationship with Jessica. She was absolutely 100 percent right about that.

And as much as he wanted to, he could not hand those finishes off to someone else. It would be cowardly. And he sensed it would leave him with a sense of incompletion that he could never outdistance.

He would go over there, and he would do all the fixes on the list in his pocket, and then they would get a real estate agent in to appraise the place, and then they would put a for-sale sign on it, and it would sell, and that last thing that held them together would be done.

And how should he feel about that?

"Happy, happy, happy," he said.

Though when Jessica had muttered that, obviously under the influence of whatever, she had looked about the furthest thing from happy! And he was aware that happy, happy, happy was about the furthest thing from how he was feeling, too.

But that just showed him how true it was and how urgent. They needed to be done. He called his assistant and did something he had not done for a long, long time.

He asked her to clear his weekend.

It wasn't until he hung up the phone that he was aware that, for someone who wanted to finish things, another motivation lurked just behind his need to fix the house.

Was Jessica going to be okay after being mugged? Not her arm. That would heal. But her. She had always had that artistic temperament, ultrasensitive to the world.

If he knew Jessica—and he did—she was not nearly as brave as she was trying to be.

So, on Saturday morning, feeling a little foolish in his brand-new tool belt, Kade knocked on the door of the house he had shared with Jessica. He was certain she had said she would be at work, but she opened the door.

He could see why she wasn't at work. She would scare people away from her fledgling business in the getup she had on. She was wearing a crazy sleeveless dress that was at least four sizes too large for her.

But, in truth, it was her face that worried him. Just as he suspected, her drawn features hinted she might not be doing well. There was the gaunt look of sleeplessness about her, as well as dark circles under her eyes.

"It's a maternity dress. I have three of them." Her tone was defensive. "They're easy to get on. See the buttons down the front? That is a very hard thing to find in a dress."

"I didn't say anything." Her arm was in the sling. At least she was following doctor's orders.

"But getting dressed was not that easy, even with the buttons. I'm running late."

He noticed her cast had been decorated with all kinds of signatures and drawings.

In college, she had always been surrounded by friends. But then marriage had done something to her. Her world, increasingly, had become about him and their house. When the pregnancy quest had begun, Jessica had quit the job she'd had since earning her arts degree. Admittedly, it had not been the best job. She had barely made minimum wage at that funky, fledgling art gallery in east Calgary.

At first, he'd liked it that Jessica was home, and doted on him. He'd liked it quite a lot, actually. Maybe he'd liked it enough he'd encouraged it. Who didn't want to come home to fresh-baked bread, or roast beef and Yorkshire pudding or three dozen chocolate-chip cookies still warm out of the oven?

Who didn't want to come home to the most beautiful woman in the world waiting for him, with some newly inventive way of showing she loved him? Once it had been rose petals floating in a freshly drawn tub. Another time it had been a candlelit wine tasting in the back garden, a garden that she had single-handedly wrested from a weedy demise.

But slowly, all her devotion had begun to grate on him. He was so aware that Jessica's world was becoming smaller and smaller: paint colors for rooms rather than canvases. She was always trying new recipes. She discovered shopping online and was constantly discovering useless bric-a-brac that he was supposed to share her enthusiasm for.

It had pierced even his colossal self-centeredness that she was becoming a shadow of the vibrant person she had once been. The obsession with the baby had just intensified the sense he didn't know who she was anymore.

She'd started buying things for a baby they didn't have: little shoes just too adorable to pass up, hand-crocheted samplers for the walls of a nursery they didn't have yet. The magazine racks—God forbid a magazine was left conveniently out—were stuffed with parenting magazines.

She was forever showing him articles on the best baby bottles, and strollers, and car seats. She wanted him to go over fabric samples with her because she had found a seamstress to custom make the crib bedding. But it didn't matter which one he picked. The next day she had more for him to look at. She was acquiring a collection of stuffed animals that would soon need a room of their own, not to mention require them to take out a second mortgage to pay for them all.

"Jessica," he remembered shouting at her, "nobody pays three hundred dollars for a teddy bear."

She had looked crushed, and then unrepentant.

The anger, he knew in retrospect, though he had no idea at the time, had nothing to do with the teddy bear. It had to do with the fact he felt responsible for the awful metamorphosis taking place in her. It had to do with the fact that he was aware, in her eyes, he was not enough for her.

She brought him back to the present. "You didn't have to say anything about the dress. I can see in your face how you feel about it."

He was fairly certain it was the memory of the three-hundred-dollar-teddy-bear fight that had been in his face, so he tried to banish those thoughts and stay in the moment. "I'm not sure why you would wear something so… er…unflattering."

"Because I don't care what you think, that's why!"

Or, he thought looking at her, she was trying very, very hard to make it appear that she didn't care what he thought.

CHAPTER EIGHT

"I LIKE THE CAST, THOUGH," Kade told Jessica.

And he did. He liked it that she had a bigger world again. All the scribbling on the cast was evidence of friends and coworkers and a life beyond the house. Okay, it grated a bit that she had managed to make a bigger world without him, and somehow it was still about babies.

"The dress is what I could get on by myself. See? Buttons down the front."

"About the dress," he said, deadpan. "Are they all that color? What would you call that color?"

"Pink?" she suggested.

"Nausea, heartburn, indigestion..." It was the slogan of a famously pink stomach-relief medication.

"The other ones are worse—"

"No, no, they can't be."

"Spiced pumpkin and real-woods camo."

"A camo maternity dress? I guess my next question would be, how are sales?"

"They are very, very popular."

"Tell me it ain't so," he groaned.

"They are part of an extraoversize line."

"Look, you are scaring me with the visual."

"Well, your visual is a little scary, too," she said, standing back from the door to let him by her. "A tool belt? And what is that you're driving?"

"I borrowed a truck."

"A truck worthy of a camo-wearing pregnant lady, too."

"I needed it for the vibrating floor sander I rented to refinish the floors."

"A floor sander. The scariness increases. You always thought we should just replace the floors," she reminded him.

"You always thought we should refinish them."

"But it doesn't matter now!" she said, but it felt as if it did. It felt as if it was part of all that was unfinished. In the house, and between them. But Kade did not tell her that.

"What do you know about refinishing a floor?" she asked, looking at her watch.

"Oh, ye of little faith," he said. "I went on the internet. It's easier than you think."

Jessica looked insultingly doubtful.

"I think that refinishing will be less time-consuming than ripping out the old floor and putting down a new one," he told her. He didn't add it might be more in keeping with his skill set.

"Why are you tackling it? Why didn't you just hire someone? That guy you hired to install my door was excellent. By the way, I owe you some money for that."

"Yeah, whatever."

She looked as if she was going to argue, but then remembered she already was in the middle of one argument with him and decided to stick to that one. "I mean this is not exactly your line of work, Kade. It's certainly not in keeping with your current lifestyle."

"What lifestyle is that?" he asked her.

"You know."

"I don't."

"CEO—chief everything officer—at a prestigious company, resident of River's Edge."

"I already told you I work all the time."

"That's exactly what I'm trying to say. You work all the time, and not at renovations. You have a very sophisticated lifestyle. You move in very high-powered circles. I don't understand why you want to do this."

"I started it," he said grimly. "And I'm going to finish it."

She looked at him, and he knew she got it. She got it at every level that he had meant it at.

"Well, I'd love to stay and help—"

He could tell she meant it to sound sarcastic, but instead they both heard the wistfulness there, and Jessica blushed.

"—but I have to go to work. It already took me nearly forty-five minutes longer to get ready than I thought it would, and my part-time staffer can only stay until noon today."

"You slept in," he guessed.

Jessica looked as if she was going to protest, but then didn't. She sighed. "I had trouble sleeping."

"I thought you would."

"What? Why?"

"There aren't very many people who could walk away from being assaulted without being affected by it. And you've always been more sensitive than the average person anyway."

She smiled wanly and gave in, just a little bit, to the fact that he was her husband. He *knew* her. "I'm okay till I lie down, then I feel as if I hear glass breaking. I jump at the sound of the furnace turning on, and that tree branch outside the bedroom scraping the window. Then, since I'm awake anyway, I contemplate how to protect my shop, and hate how helpless I feel."

He drew in a deep breath. The warrior in him wanted to devote his life to protecting her.

But she looked as abashed at her confessions as he was at his reaction to them. Jessica glanced again at her watch. "Yikes! Would you look at the time! Sorry, again. I can't help."

"It doesn't matter. There is a lot of legwork before I actually do anything. I have to move furniture before I get started on the floors."

She cast a look at Behemoth. She was obviously thinking moving furniture was a two-person job, but he had also rented a dolly this morning with that recliner specifically in mind.

But Jessica surprised him. The practicalities of moving furniture were not what was on her mind.

"Remember the day we brought that home?" she asked softly.

These were the conversations he didn't want to have. Because the truth was that he remembered everything.

"You protesting the whole way home how ugly it was," Kade reminded her. He thought her exact words had been that it didn't fit with her *vision* for their house. He hadn't become totally jaded with the vision yet. Or maybe he had started to, because he had brought home the chair over her strenuous protests.

"And then we couldn't get it in the door. It weighs about a thousand pounds—"

"Well, maybe fifty," he corrected her wryly.

"And I was trying to hold up one end of it and you were trying to stuff it through the door. I told you it was a sign the house did not want it, and then you shoved extrahard. The frame of the door cracked and Behemoth catapulted into the house and nearly crushed me."

"Except I saved you," he said.

She looked at his face. Her eyes were very wide. She looked as if she was going to step toward him.

Suddenly, he remembered how they had celebrated getting that chair into the house. On the chair. And she had seemed affectionately tolerant of Behemoth after that.

The memory was between them, liquid and white-hot. It didn't mean anything that she still had the chair, did it?

"Go to work," Kade said gruffly, deliberately stepping back from her. "You probably wouldn't be of any help in your delicate state anyway."

Too late, he realized that a delicate state usually referred to pregnancy, and that, of course, was the topic that was a minefield between them.

Thankfully, she seemed a little rattled, as he was himself, by the Behemoth memory. He didn't intend to share the secret of the furniture-moving dolly with her. She would come home, and the floors would be completely done, and the furniture back in place and she would be filled with complete admiration for his adeptness in all things masculine.

And she would be so sorry things had not worked between them.

That thought blasted through his brain from nowhere that he could discern.

"Where should I put the furniture?" he asked hastily.

"Oh. Good question. Try the guest room. I use it as an office. It probably has the most room in it right now."

"Okay."

She cast one last rather insultingly doubtful look around the living room, but then looked at her watch and made a squeaking noise. She disappeared and came back in a few minutes, her look improved ever so slightly by a nice handbag, ultrahigh heels and dark glasses that hid the circles under her eyes.

"All right," she called. "Good luck. See you later."

Then she turned and, with her heels clacking sexy defiance of that horrible dress, went through the kitchen and out the back door. The door seemed to snap shut behind her. Was he mistaken, or had she been eager to get away from him?

Jessica could not wait to get out of that house! Her husband was an attractive man. His executive look—the tailored suits and linen shirts and silk ties, the manicured nails and the beautifully groomed hair—was enough to make any woman give him a second glance.

And yet the man he was this morning felt like *her* Kade. Casual in jeans faded to nearly white, his plaid shirt open at the beautiful column of his throat, his sleeves rolled up over the carved muscle of his forearms, a faint shadow of whiskers on his face. It was who he had been in private—dressed down, relaxed, so, so sexy.

Add to that the tool belt riding low on his hips, his easy confidence about pitting all that masculine strength against Behemoth…

Behemoth. Back in the day. When everything was still *fun*.

Good grief, she had wanted to just throw

herself against him this morning, feel his heart beating beneath her cheek, feel his arms close around her.

The robbery had left her far more rattled than she ever could have believed. Her sleep was troubled. She started at the least sound. Her mind drifted back to that morning if she let down her guard for even a second. And she felt dreadfully alone with the stress of it.

It was making her weak. The fact that he *knew* how she would react made her lonely for him, even though the sane part of her knew wanting to lean on Kade was an insane form of weakness. She had already tried that once, and he wasn't good at comforting her. Probably what had stopped her from throwing herself at him this morning was uncertainty. Would he have gathered her to him, rested his chin on the top of her head, folded his arms around her? Or would he, after an uncomfortable moment of tolerating her embrace, have stepped away?

She did not think it would be a good idea to make herself vulnerable to Kade again.

But even with that resolve strong within her, Jessica arrived at work feeling rattled.

Her stomach was in knots.

"Good grief," said Macy, her part-time

staffer, stopping in her tracks. "Where'd you get that dress?"

"You know perfectly well I got it from the rack of Poppy Puppins at the back."

"It looks horrible on you."

Jessica didn't want to look horrible. She hated it that Kade had seen her looking horrible, even though she had deliberately worn the outfit to let him know she did not care one whit what he thought of her.

Sleep deprivation, obviously, was kicking in, plus it was some kind of reaction to being the victim of a crime, just as Kade had said, because Jessica felt as if she was fighting not to burst into tears.

"It has buttons on the front!" Jessica exclaimed for the second time that day. Ignoring the pitying look from Macy, she headed to office and slammed the door behind her.

She could not focus, even before she had *the* thought. *The* thought made her stomach feel as if it had become the lead car on the world's biggest roller coaster. It plunged downward and then did a crazy double loop. She bolted out of her office and into the store.

"Jessica? What's wrong?"

Jessica stared at Macy, not really seeing her. This was the thought that was tormenting her:

Had she told Kade to put the furniture in the guest room? But she used that room as an office! And if she was not mistaken, she had the names of adoption agencies and lawyers who specialized in that field strewn all over the desk.

"Are you okay?" Macy asked. She dropped a tiny stuffed football and rushed to Jessica's side. "Are you going to faint?"

Jessica looked down at the bill of lading she still had clutched in her hand. She did feel terribly wobbly. "I think I'm okay," she said doubtfully.

"I was supposed to babysit for my sister at noon, but if you want, I'll see if my mom can do it instead."

Jessica was ashamed that her distress, her weakness, was that obvious to her employee. But her soon-to-be ex-husband had always had a gift for rattling her world, in one way or another.

What did it matter if he knew she was contemplating adoption? But at some deep, deep level, she did not want him to know.

So though usually Jessica would have said a vehement no to an offer like Macy had just made, she didn't. Usually, she would have pulled herself together. She could just phone and tell Kade to put Behemoth in her bedroom instead of the office.

She looked at her watch. He'd been there, in her house, for an hour and a half. It was possible he was already in the office, poring over her personal papers, uncovering her secrets.

"Oh, Macy, could you? I'd be so grateful." She shoved the bill of lading into Macy's hand.

And it wasn't until Jessica was halfway home that she realized she had not even waited for Macy's answer, but had bolted out the door as if her house was on fire.

Which, in less than half an hour, it would be.

CHAPTER NINE

JESSICA PULLED UP to the front of her house. She usually parked in the back, but such was her sense of urgency, she had decided to cut seconds by parking out front instead.

Her sense of her life spiraling out of her control deepened at what awaited her. All the living room furniture was on the front lawn, with the exception of Behemoth, which, as she already knew, could not fit through the front door. At least she hoped the furniture on the front lawn indicated there had been no invasion of her office.

Gathering herself, Jessica went up the steps. The front door to her house was open. She peered in. Her living room was emptied of furniture.

Kade was glaring down at some instructions in his hand. There was a machine there that looked like a huge floor polisher, only it had a bag attached to it, like a lawn mower. Though it felt like further weakness, she stood there for a minute regarding him, loving the look of him.

He looked big and broad and strong. He looked like the kind of man every woman dreamed of leaning on. But that was what Jessica needed to remember.

When she had needed someone to lean on, and when that person should have been her husband? Kade had not been there. At first he had just been emotionally absent, but then he had begun working longer and longer hours, until he was physically absent, too.

By the time Kade had made it official and moved out, her abandonment by her husband had already been complete.

Remembering all that as a defense against how glorious he looked right now, Jessica cleared her throat.

"It's not for sale," he said, without looking up.

"What?"

He did look up then. "What are you doing back?" he asked with a frown.

"What's not for sale?"

"The furniture. People keep stopping and asking if there's a yard sale. The coffee table is generating quite a lot of interest."

"I always told you it was a good piece."

He was silent for a moment. She knew she had left herself wide-open for him to tease her about what a *good piece* meant to him as opposed to what it meant to her. When he didn't follow that thread—once he had found teasing her irresistible—she was not sure how she felt. But it was not relieved.

"If Behemoth was out there," Kade said, "people would be throwing their money at me. I'd be at the center of a bidding war. The newspaper would probably be here by now to find out what all the fuss on Twenty-Ninth Avenue was about."

"Which brings me to my next question," Jessica said. "Why exactly is everything out on the lawn?"

He lifted a shoulder. "Faster to toss it out there than move it all down the hall."

"Toss?" she said.

"I meant gently move."

Despite the fact it meant he had been careless with her possessions, no matter what he said—and what was to stop anyone from taking whatever they wanted?—she felt relief that he had obviously not been anywhere near the spare bedroom that served as her office. She would know by looking at him if he had seen

that adoption stuff, but obviously he was pre-
occupied with the machine in front of him.

It didn't surprise her that he would throw her
things out on the lawn if that was faster than
maneuvering them down the hallway. He had
always had intensity of focus. When he wanted
something, he simply removed the obstacles to
getting it. It had made him a tremendous success in business.

It was how he had wooed her. She had been
bowled over by him. But then that same attitude had become a toxin in their relationship.

A baby wasn't going to happen? Cut your
losses and move on.

"How come you're home?" he asked again.

"Things were slow," she, who never told a
fib, lied with shocking ease. "I shut it down a
bit early. It seemed to me I should be helping
out here. After all, I started it, too."

"I don't really see how you can help. You're
kind of handicapped at the moment." He regarded her with a furrowed brow. "You still
look not quite right. Pale. Fragile."

"I'm fine."

He brightened as he thought of a use for her.
"I know what you could do! You could order
pizza. Is Stradivarius still around the corner?

God, I've missed that pizza. I haven't had it since—"

His voice trailed away. *Since you left me.* Had he missed her? At all? Or had even pizza rated higher than her?

It didn't matter. Their lives were separate now. She was moving on. Which reminded her of why she had rushed home. And it was not to order him a pizza!

She sidled by Kade. She passed close enough to him to breath in the wonderful familiar scent of him, mixed with something unfamiliar. Sawdust from the floor?

It was tempting to lean just a little closer and breathe deeply of the intoxication that was his scent. But she didn't.

"I'll just go, um, freshen up." She didn't mean changing her clothes. Changing clothes had become a rather daunting undertaking with one arm out of commission. What she really meant was she would go to her office and put her life away from his prying eyes just in case he did make it in there.

Behemoth, it turned out, was in the bathroom, not her office. It would be necessary to climb over it if she was really freshening up, which she wasn't. How far did she need to take the ruse? Did she need to climb over that thing and flush the toilet?

It seemed as if it would be endangering her other arm, and unnecessarily, because when she glanced back down the hall, Kade was not paying the least bit of attention to her.

As always.

The thought was edged with so much bitterness she could practically taste it, like chewing on a lemon peel.

Jessica went into her office. The papers were all out, just as she had remembered, but they were undisturbed. She slid them into the top drawer of the desk. She considered locking it, but it fell under the category of him not paying any attention to her. She doubted Kade would find her interesting enough to pry into her closed desk.

"Interesting placement of Behemoth," she said when she came back into the living room.

"I was thinking it might start a trend. Every man would like a recliner in the bathroom. Some kind of recliner-toilet combination is probably a million-dollar idea just waiting to be developed."

"That is gross."

"It isn't. It's combining practicality with extreme luxury. You have to admit there is nothing particularly comfortable or luxurious about a toilet seat."

She remembered this about him with an ache of longing: that easy irreverence that made her want to be stuffy and disapproving, but she always gave in and laughed instead.

She could feel her lips twitching. He saw it, too.

"Think about it," Kade pressed on. "We could offer designer colors. Pickled pumpkin and redneck camo. We could throw in a free matching dress with every purchase."

She tried to be stern. She giggled. He smiled at her giggle. She succeeded in smothering her giggle. He succeeded in smothering his smile.

"I think," she said severely, Mother Superior to misbehaving novice, "we should try to get the floors done before we tackle anything else together."

"Oh, right. Okay. So come and look at this."

She went over to where he was glaring at the floor. "What do you think?"

"About what?"

"That was what I was afraid of," he groaned. "I already sanded this part. Not much is happening. I just went out and got a different grit of sandpaper. I'm going to try it again. Cover your ears."

Obediently, Jessica put her hands over her ears. The machine roared to life. It was like standing next to a jackhammer.

To her relief, Kade stopped it after a few seconds. "Better," he said, "but still…" A light came on in his face. "It's not heavy enough."

"Huh?"

"The sander. It isn't heavy enough to really dig into those floors. Get on."

"What?"

"Come on. Sit on the front of it."

"Have you lost your mind?"

"You wanted to help. You can't do much with your arm like that. Come sit on the sander."

Why hadn't she just gone and ordered a pizza? Against her better judgment, she moved a little closer. "Sit on it?" She tapped it. "Here?"

He nodded eagerly.

Oh, jeez, it had always been hard not to get caught up in his enthusiasm.

She kicked off her shoes, gathered her skirt underneath her and sat down regally on the sander. She planted her feet firmly on a part of it that looked like a front fender. "Do not do anything that will jeopardize my other arm," she warned him.

"Don't worry." Grinning happily, he started

the sander. A quiver ran through her. And then a tremble.

"Oh, my God." Her voice came out shaking, as if she was trying to talk from under water. In the midst of an earthquake. With her good hand, she clutched wildly at the side of the sander. She braced her front feet.

"Ready?"

Ready? *Sheesh, Jessica, run for your life!* Instead, she clung like a bronc rider waiting for the gate to open. She nodded her head.

The machine lurched across the floor.

"That's better," Kade called. "It's working!" He swung the huge machine slowly back and forth over the floor.

"I feel like I'm on one of those machines from a seventies gym," she yelled. Her voice sounded as if she was a cartoon character. Her whole body was vibrating crazily. She could see the flesh on her arms and legs jiggling rapidly.

She started to laugh. Even her laughter was shaking. Kade also gave a shout of pure glee.

He abandoned the slow sweeping motions in the corner and swiveled the machine outward. He raced across the living room, pushing the machine in front of him. Jessica glanced over her shoulder. A wide swath of sanded wood showed behind them, like the wake behind a boat.

They rocketed toward the front door.

An older woman put her head in. Her glasses slipped down her face and her mouth fell open. She was followed by her husband. His mouth fell open, and he grabbed her arm and tried to push her back out the door, as if protecting her from a sight unsuitable for a lady.

She was having none of it, though. She stood her ground, taking in the sight, wide-eyed.

Kade jerked the machine to a halt so quickly Jessica was nearly launched. He turned off the machine. Jessica pulled her skirt down—the vibrating had made it ride dangerously up her thigh—and tried to quit laughing. An undignified snort, caused by the suppressed laughter, came out of her mouth.

"Yes?" Kade asked their visitors, his voice dignified, as if not a thing was amiss.

"Uh, we were wondering if there's a yard sale," the man said when it was evident his wife was still shocked speechless. "We wondered about the bench."

"Not for sale," Kade said, and then Jessica heard a familiar wickedness enter his tone.

"However, I'll give you a good deal on the world's best vibrator."

The woman staggered backward out the door. The man's mouth fell open so hard, his chin hit his chest.

"Sorry to disturb you," he cried as he backed out the door after his wife.

Jessica waited until they were gone. She glared up at the man who was her husband, but she could not stir any genuine annoyance with him. Instead, she remembered how funny and spontaneous he was, she remembered that irreverent edge to his humor.

A smile was tickling his lips. And then she remembered that oh-so-familiar grin. And realized she had never really forgotten that.

Kade gave a shout of pure delight and devilment. And then the laughter spilled out of Jessica, too, and they were both laughing. Hard. Until they were doubled over with it, until the walls of their little house rang with it.

Until the laughter flowed between them like a river that connected them to everything they had once been.

CHAPTER TEN

KADE LOOKED AT Jessica and realized how much he loved to make her laugh. He always had. That was what he had missed most when their relationship had begun to go sideways. Her laughter.

"Goodness," Jessica said a little breathlessly. "I have not laughed like that in a very long time."

"Me, either," he admitted.

"It reminds me of when we were younger," she said.

"Me, too."

"Before…" Her voice faded away. But he knew what she meant. Before the loss of the first baby. And then the second one. Her laughter had leached out of her like bloodred wine leaking from a wineskin with a small puncture in it.

And when she had stopped laughing, and when he had realized how powerless he was to fix that, nothing had seemed worth laughing about to him anymore, either.

Now he watched as she scrambled off the sander, brushing at that ugly skirt with her good arm. The laughter had lightened the strained look around her eyes and mouth.

But when she faced him, a different kind of strain was there. And it wasn't, for once, the strain of remembering everything that had transpired between them.

This had been lost, too, this deep and delicious sense of awareness of each other. Or maybe not lost. Maybe it had gone underground, like a creek that ran below the surface. It didn't matter that right now, Jessica's surface was encased in that thoroughly revolting dress. Kade could see, with utter ease, to what was underneath. And not her underwear. Her spirit. He could sense that beautiful, sensual awareness of each other, a longing to touch and explore.

In their marriage, it felt as if that had gone, too. It had gone the same place the laughter had gone—into that lonely abyss. It was as if the raft of life that they had shared had snapped in two, and they had stood by helplessly, with no paddles, drifting farther and farther away, not able to stop it.

"Why babies?" he asked softly.

"What?"

She actually looked frightened by the question.

"Why Baby Boomer? Why is your business about all things baby when that caused us so much heartache?"

"Oh." She relaxed visibly. "I'm not sure it was even intentional. You know some of my friends had seen the nursery you and I—" Her voice drifted away and she squinted, as if looking at something in the distance. Then she cleared her throat. "Nicole Reynolds asked me if I could do something for her. A mural on the wall of her nursery. It was a forest scene, with rabbits and birds and a deer. It was an immersion and it kind of snatched me back from the brink. Gave me purpose and a reason to get up in the morning. I liked being part of what was happening in their family, that circle of joy and expectation. It just kind of snowballed."

He was so aware he had caused her that pain. Well, not all of it. The miscarriages had put her in a space he couldn't reach. And then she'd wanted to try again. To plunge herself into that pool of misery he could not rescue her from again. He'd thought it was his job to make her happy. To make her world perfect.

At some point, to his grave detriment, he had given up trying.

"I'm sorry, Jessie. I'm sorry it wasn't me who snatched you back from the brink."

Her eyes skittered to him and then away. For a moment it looked as if she would cross that abyss between them, throw herself into his embrace, come home.

But that moment passed even before he recognized completely what was blooming inside him.

Hope.

Shouldn't he know by now that that was the worst trap of all? To hope?

She seemed to recognize it, because smiling way too brightly, she said, "How about if I go order that pizza now?"

"Oh, yeah, sure."

She retreated to the kitchen; he looked at the floors. With the extra weight on the sander, wood had disappeared quickly. The wood was bare, but wavy. If he put a level on it, it would probably rock like the little horse in one of her nursery displays. He was fairly certain that the damage caused by her wild ride on the sander was something wood filler could not fix.

But he was aware of *liking* this kind of problem over the other kind. The baffling problems of the heart.

"What kind of pizza?" she called.

"The usual," he said, before he remembered they really didn't have a usual anymore, not since their lives had become unusual.

But she didn't miss a beat, and he heard her talking into the phone, ordering a half pepperoni and mushroom and a half anchovies and pineapple and ham.

He went into the kitchen and watched her. The afternoon sunshine was painting her in gold. Even in that horrible dress, she looked beautiful. He remembered what it was to share a life with her and felt the pang of intense loss.

And suspected she was feeling it, too. Jessica had hung up the phone, but she had all the old take-out menus out of the kitchen drawer—she'd actually allowed them to have a junk drawer—and was studying them hard.

"You're too heavy," he said when she glanced up at him.

"Excuse me? Then maybe pizza isn't the right choice!"

"Oh, for heaven's sake. Not like that."

"Not like what?"

"You," he said, and could hear the gruff sincerity in his voice, "are perfect. You are too heavy for the sander! We dug some pretty good ruts in the floor."

"Oh." She blushed and looked back at the menus. She was pleased that he thought she was perfect. And he was pleased that he had pleased her, even though the road they were on seemed fraught with danger. "You should have hired it out."

"Very unmanly," he said.

"You," she said, and he could hear the sincerity in her voice, "couldn't be unmanly if you were wearing this dress."

He was pleased that she thought he was manly, though the sense of danger was hissing in the air between them now.

She was right, and not just about the manly part. He should have hired the floor job out. The truth, he wouldn't have missed those moments of her laughter for the world. Even if the floor was completely wrecked, which seemed like a distinct possibility at the moment, that seemed a small price to pay.

"I just need something lighter than you to put on the sander." He deliberately walked away from the building tension between them and went out the back door to their toolshed. He found an old cinder block. He didn't miss the look on her face when he came back in hefting it, as her eyes found the bulge of his biceps and lingered there for a heated moment.

He slowed marginally, liking her admiration of his manliness more than he had a right to. Then he went into the living room and found and pitted himself against a nice comforting problem, one that he could solve. How did you get a cinder block to sit on a sander?

Kade finally had it attached, and restarted the machine. It wasn't nearly as much fun as waltzing around the room with Jessica. And it wasn't nearly as dangerous, either.

Or that was what he thought until the precise moment he smelled smoke. Frowning, he looked toward the kitchen. They were having pizza. What was she burning?

He shut off the sander, and went into the kitchen doorway, expecting crazily to find her pulling burned cookies from the oven. She had gone through a cookie phase when she had made her world all about him. Who had known there were so many kinds of cookies?

Once or twice, he had tried to distract her from her full-scaled descent into domestic divahood. He had crossed the kitchen, breathed on her neck, nibbled her ear…

He remembered them laughing when he'd lured her away and they'd come back to cookies burned black. She had taken them out of the oven and thrown the whole sheet out into the yard…

But now there were no cookies. In fact, Jessica was standing right where he had left her, still studying all the take-out menus as if each one represented something very special. Which it did, not that he wanted to go there now. Kade did not want to remember Chinese food on the front steps during a thunderstorm, or a memorable evening of naked pad thai, a real dish that they had eaten, well, in the spirit of the name.

"Don't distract me," he snapped at her, and that earned him a wide-eyed look of surprise.

"What are you burning?"

"I'm not burning anything."

He turned away from her, sniffing the air. It wasn't coming from in here, the kitchen. In fact, it seemed to be coming from the living room. He turned back in and the sanding machine caught his attention. A wisp of something curled out of the bag that caught the sawdust coming off the floor.

And in the split second that he was watching it, that wisp of phantom gray turned into a belch of pure black smoke.

"The house is on fire!" he cried.

"That's not funny," she said.

He pushed by her and opened the cupboard by the stove—thank God she had not moved things around—and picked up the huge canner stored there. He dashed to the sink, then remembered the canner didn't fit well under the faucet. He tilted it precariously and turned on the water. It seemed it was filling in slow motion.

She sniffed the air. "What the—"

He glanced back at the door between the kitchen and the living room. A cloud of black smoke billowed in, up close to the top of the door frame.

"Get out of the house," he yelled at her. He picked up the pot and raced out to the living room. The first flame was just shooting out of the sawdust bag on the sander. He threw the pot of water on it. The fire crackled, and then disappeared into a cloud of thick black smoke that was so acrid smelling he choked on it.

He threw the pot on the floor, and went to Jessica, who, surprise, surprise, had not followed his instructions and had not bolted for the door and the safety of the backyard. She was still standing by the menus with her mouth open.

He scooped her up. He was not sure how he managed to think of her arm under these circumstances, but he did and he was extracareful not to put any pressure on her injured limb. He tucked her close to his chest—and felt a sense, despite the awful urgency of this situation, of being exactly where he belonged.

Protecting Jessica, looking after her, using his superior strength to keep her safe. She was stunned into silence, her green eyes wide and startled on his face.

And then he felt something sigh within her and knew she felt it, too. That somehow she belonged here, in his arms.

He juggled her to get the back door open, then hurtled down the back steps and into the yard. With reluctance, he let her slide from his arms and find her own feet.

"Is the house on fire?" she asked. "Should I call 911?"

"I want you to make note of the technique. First, you get to a safe place, then you call 911."

"But the phone's in there."

"I have one," he tapped his pocket. "But don't worry. The fire's out. I just didn't want you breathing that black guck into your lungs."

"My hero," she said drily. "Rescuing me from the fire you started."

"It wasn't exactly a fire," he said.

She lifted an eyebrow at him.

"A smolder. Prefire at best."

"Ah."

"The sander must be flawed. Sheesh. We could sue them. I'm going to call them right now and let them know the danger they have put us in." He called the rental company. He started to blast them, but then stopped and listened.

He hung up the phone and hung his head.

"What?"

Kade did not want to admit this, but he choked it out. "My fault. You need to check the finish that was on the floor before you start sanding. Some of the finishes become highly flammable if you add friction."

She was smiling at him as if it didn't matter one bit. "You've always been like that," she said. "Just charge ahead, to hell with the instructions."

"And I'm often left cleaning up messes of my own making," he said. "I'm going to go back into the house. You stay out here. Toxins."

"It's not as if I'm pregnant," she said, and he heard the faint bitterness and the utter defeat in those words.

And there it was, the ultrasensitive topic between them. There was nothing to say. He had already said everything he knew how to say. If it was meant to be, it would be. Maybe if they relaxed. It didn't change how he felt about her. He didn't care about a baby. He cared about her.

So he had said everything he could say on that topic, most if it wrong.

And so now he said nothing at all. He just laid his hand on her cheek, and held it there for a moment, hoping she could *feel* what he had never been able to say.

CHAPTER ELEVEN

Jessica did seem to be able to feel all those things he had never been able to say, because instead of slapping his hand away, she leaned into it, and then covered it with her own, and closed her eyes. She sighed, and then opened her eyes, and it seemed to him it was with reluctance she put his hand away from her.

And so they went into the house together and paused in the doorway.

"Wow, does that stink," Jessica said. She went and grabbed a couple of dish towels off the oven handle. "We need these over our faces, not that I can tie them."

Kade took the towels from her and tied one over the bottom half of her face and one over his.

"Is mine manly?" he asked. "Or did I get the one with the flowers on it?"

He saw her eyes smile from under her mask.

Now Jessica was in an ugly dress *and* had her face covered up. But the laughter still twinkled around the edges of her eyes, and it made her so beautiful it threatened to take his breath away far more than the toxic cloud of odor in the room.

Firmly, Kade made himself turn from her, and aware he looked ridiculous, like an old-time bandito, surveyed the damage to the living room.

All that was left of the sander bag was ribbons of charred fabric. They were still smoking, so he went over and picked up the sander and threw it out the front door, possibly with a little more force than was necessary. It hit the concrete walkway and pieces shot off it and scattered.

"That gave me a manly sense of satisfaction," Kade said, his voice muffled from under the dish towel. He turned back into the room.

The smile deepened around her eyes. How was this that they had narrowly averted disaster, and yet it felt good to be with her? It was as if a wall that had been erected between them was showing signs of stress, a brick or two falling out of it.

There was a large scorch mark on the floor where the sander had been, and a black ugly film shining with some oily substance coated the floor where he had thrown the water. The smoke had belched up and stained the ceiling.

"I think the worst damage is the smell," Kade said. "It's awful, like a potent chemical soup. I don't think you're going to be able to stay here until it airs out a bit."

"It's okay. I'll get a hotel."

"You're probably going to have to call your insurance company. The smell is probably through the whole house. Your clothes have probably absorbed it."

"Oh, boy," she said, "two claims in one week. What do you suppose that will do to my premiums?" And then she giggled. "It's a good thing the furniture is on the lawn. It won't have this smell in it. Do you think I'm going to have to repaint?"

"You don't have to go to a hotel," he said. "I've got lots of room."

Son, I say, son, what are you doing?

She hesitated. There was a knock at the door.

"Pizza," they said together.

Jessica contemplated what she was feeling as Kade looked after the pizza delivery. He cocked his head slightly at her, a signal to look at the delivery boy, who was oblivious, earbuds in, head bobbing. He didn't seem to even notice that he was stepping over a smoldering piece of machinery on the front walkway to get to the door. If he noticed the smell rolling out of the house, it did not affect his rhythm in any way.

As they watched the pizza boy depart, she felt like laughing again. That was impossible! She'd had two disasters in one week. She should be crying, not feeling as if an effervescent bubble of joy was rising in her.

Shock, she told herself. She was reacting to the pure shock of life delivering the unexpected. Wasn't there something just a little bit delightful about being surprised?

"Of course I can't stay with you, Kade," she said, coming to her senses, despite the shock of being surprised. "I'll get a hotel room. Or I can stay with friends."

"Why don't we go to my place and eat the pizza? You don't make your best decisions on an empty stomach. We'll figure it out from there."

Other than the fact it, once again, felt good to be *known*, that sounded so reasonable. She was hungry, and it would be better to look for a place to live for the next few days on a full tummy. What would it hurt to go to his place to have the pizza? She had to admit that she was curious about where Kade lived.

And so she found herself heading for the borrowed truck, laughing at the irony of him carefully locking the door when all her furniture was still on the lawn. Except for her precious bench, which at the last moment, she made him load into the box of the truck, they just left everything there.

She suspected leaving her furniture on the lawn was not nearly as dangerous as getting into that truck with him and heading toward a peek at his life.

His condo building sat in the middle of a parklike setting in a curve in the Bow River. Everything about the building, including its prime nearly downtown location, whispered class, wealth and arrival. There was a waterfall feature in the center of the circular flagstone driveway. The building was faced in black granite and black tinted glass, and yet was saved from the coldness of pure modern design by the seamless blending of more rustic elements such as stone and wood in the very impressive facade.

A uniformed doorman came out when Kade pulled up in front of the posh entryway to the building.

"Hey, Samuel, can you park this in the secured visitor area for me?"

Kade came and helped her out of the truck, and she was aware of the gurgle of the waterfall sliding over rocks. Something in the plantings around it smelled wonderful. Honeysuckle?

If the doorman was surprised to have a pickup truck to park among the expensive sports cars and luxury vehicles, it certainly didn't show in his smooth features.

"It's underground," Kade said to Jessica, when the truck had pulled away. "You don't have to worry about your bench."

The truth was she was so bowled over by her surroundings, the bench had slipped her mind.

Though the incredible landscape outside should have prepared her for the lobby, she felt unprepared. The entryway to the building was gorgeous, with soaring ceilings, a huge chandelier and deep distressed-leather sofas grouped around a fireplace.

No wonder he had never come home.

"Wow," Jessica said, gulping. "Our little place must seem pretty humble after this. I can see why you were just going to give it to me."

Kade looked around, as if he was puzzled. "I actually didn't pick the place," he said. "The company owns several units in here that we use for visiting executives. One was available. I needed a place to go and we had one vacant. I rent it from the company."

She cast him a glance as they took a quiet elevator up to the top floor. He really did seem oblivious to the sumptuous surroundings he found himself in. Once off the elevator, Kade put a code into the keyless entry.

"It's 1121," he said, "in case you ever need it."

She ducked her head at the trust he had in her—gosh, what if she barged in when he was entertaining a girlfriend?—and because it felt sad that she knew she would never need it. Well, unless she did stay for a couple of days until the disaster at her place was sorted.

Already, she realized with wry self-knowledge, her vehement no to his invitation was wavering.

Maybe that wasn't so surprising. Kade was charming, and he could be lethally so. She needed to remember charm was not something you could take to the bank in a relationship.

He opened the door and stood back.

"Oh, my gosh," Jessica said, stepping by him. The sense of being seduced, somehow, increased. She found herself standing in a wide entryway, floored in huge marble tiles. That area flowed seamlessly into the open-space living area, where floor-to-ceiling windows

looked out over the park and pathways that surrounded the Bow River.

The views were breathtaking and exquisite,
and she had a sense of being intensely curious
and not knowing where to look first, because
the interior of the apartment was also breathtaking. The furnishings and finishes were ul-
tramodern and high-end. The kitchen, on the
back wall of the huge open space, was a masterpiece of granite and stainless steel. A huge
island had the cooktop in it, and a space-age
stainless-steel fan over that.

"Let's eat," Kade said. He'd obviously gotten used to all this luxury. The fabulous interior of his apartment didn't create even a ripple
in him. "Maybe on the deck? It's a nice night.
I'll just get some plates."

Jessica, as if in a dream, moved out fold-back
glass doors onto the covered terrace. It was so
big it easily contained a sitting area with six
deeply cushioned dark rattan chairs grouped
together. On the other side of it sat a huge rustic plank table with dining chairs around it. It
looked as if it could sit eight people with ease.

Huge planters contained everything from
full-size trees to bashful groups of purple
pansies. She took a seat at the table and wondered about all the parties that had been hosted

here that she had not been invited to. She looked out over the river.

She felt as if she was going to cry. The apartment screamed to her that he had moved on. That he had a life she knew nothing about. After all their closeness this afternoon, she suddenly felt unbearably lonely.

Kade came out, juggling dishes and the pizza.

"What?" he said, sliding her a look as he put everything down.

"Your apartment is beautiful," she said, and could hear the stiffness in her own voice.

"Yeah, it's okay," he said. She cast him a look. Was he deliberately understating it?

"The kitchen is like something out of a magazine layout."

He shrugged, took a slice of pizza out of the box and laid it on her plate, from the pepperoni half, just as if they had ordered pizza together yesterday instead of a long, long time ago.

"I think I'll look for open concept in my next place," she said. She bit into the pizza and tried not to swoon. Not just because the pizza was so good, but because of the memories that swarmed in with the flavor.

"Don't," he said.

Swoon over pizza?

"It's not all it's cracked up to be, open concept."

"Oh," she said, relieved. "You don't like it?"

"You can't be messy. Everything's out in the open all the time. Where do you hide from your dirty dishes?"

"That would be hard on you," Jessica said. She remembered painful words between them over things that now seemed so ridiculous: toothpaste smears on the sink, the toilet paper roll put on the "wrong" way. "But I didn't see any dirty dishes."

"Oh, the condo offers a service. They send someone in to clean and make the beds and stuff. You don't think I'm keeping all those plants alive, do you?"

"Very swanky," she said. "Kind of like living at a hotel."

"Exactly. That is probably why this place," Kade said, "has never felt like home."

Jessica felt the shock of that ripple through her. This beautiful, perfect space did not feel like home to him?

"I've missed this pizza," he said.

"Me, too," she said. But she knew neither of them was talking about pizza. They sat out on his deck and watched the light change on the river as the sun went down behind them. The silence was comfortable between them.

"I should go," she finally said. "I have to make some phone calls. It's probably getting late to call a friend for tonight. I'll go to a hotel and arrange something for the rest of the week."

"You shouldn't bother. It sounds as if it's going to be a lot of hassle. There is lots of room here. There's a guest room."

Logically, Jessica knew she could not stay. But it felt so good to be here. It felt oddly like home to her, even if it didn't to Kade. Maybe it was because she was aware that, for the very first time since she had been attacked in her business, she felt safe.

And so tired. And relaxed.

Maybe for her, home was where Kade was, which was all the more reason to go, really.

"Okay," she heard herself saying, without nearly enough fight. "Maybe just for one night."

The logical part of her tried to kick in. "I should have packed a bag. I don't know why I didn't think of it."

"I told you," Kade said with an indulgent smile, "you don't think well when you're hungry. I thought of it, but then I wondered if your stuff was going to smell like that burning sander. Don't worry. Like I said, the place is set up for visiting execs. The bathrooms are all stocked up with toothbrushes and toothpaste and shampoo and stuff. And you don't need pajamas."

She could feel her eyebrows shoot up into her hairline.

He laughed. "The guest bedroom has its own en suite, not that I was suggesting you sleep naked. You can borrow one of my shirts."

Good grief, he was her husband. Why would she blush like a schoolgirl when the word *naked* fell, with such aggravating ease, from his gorgeous lips?

CHAPTER TWELVE

"AND WHAT SHOULD I do for clothes tomorrow?"
Jessica asked. Her voice felt stiff with tension.

But Kade did not seem tense at all. He just
shrugged, and then said, his tone teasing, "We
will figure something out. It's not as though we
could do worse than what you have on."

We.

She ordered herself not to give in to this. It
was a weakness to let him look after her. It was
an illusion to feel safe with him.

But she did. And she was suddenly aware
she had not really slept or even eaten properly
since the break-in. Exhaustion settled over her.

"One night," she decided. "My place will
probably be aired out by tomorrow."

"Probably," he said insincerely.

"I think I have to go to bed now."

"All right. I'll show you the way, and find
you a shirt to wear for pajamas."

"I'll put away the dishes."

"No, I'll do it. I've gotten better at picking up behind myself."

Was that true, or would the maid come and pick up after them tomorrow? She found she just didn't care. She was giving herself over to the luxurious feeling of being looked after. Just for one night, though!

And then she found herself led down a wide hallway and tucked inside a bedroom that was an opulent symphony of grays. She went into the attached bathroom. Her mouth fell open. There was a beautiful bathtub shaped like an egg in here. And double sinks and granite, and a walk-in shower. And this was the guest room.

Why did she feel such comfort that he didn't feel as at home here as he had in the humble little wreck of a house they had shared?

Just tired, she told herself. As promised, there was everything she needed there, from toothbrushes to fresh towels.

When she went out of the bathroom, she saw he had left a shirt on the bed for her. Unable to stop herself, she buried her face in it, and inhaled the deep and wonderful scent of her husband. She managed to get the oversize buttons undone on the dress and get it off.

She pulled his shirt on. His buttons weren't

quite so easy to do up, but she managed. When she noticed they were done up crooked, she didn't have the energy to change them. She tumbled into the deep luxury of that bed, looked out the window at the lights of the city reflecting in the dark waters of the river and felt her eyes grow heavy.

She realized, for the first time since her shop had been broken into and she had been injured in her ill-advised scuffle with the perpetrator, she was going to get to sleep easily. She suspected she would sleep deeply.

Only it wasn't really the first time in a week.

It was the first time in a year.

Kade was so aware that Jessica was right down the hallway from him. He wished he would not have made that crack about her sleeping naked.

Because a man did not want to be having naked thoughts about the wife he still missed and mourned.

But he had developed ways of getting by all these painful feelings. He looked at his watch. Despite the fact Jessica was in bed—she had always handled stress poorly, and he suspected she was exhausted—it was still early.

And he had his balm.

He had work. Plus, he had nearly wrecked

her house today. He needed to look after that. He liked the sense of having a mission. This time, though, he decided to call the guy who had fixed her shop door, at least for the floors.

Jake, like all good carpenters and handymen in the supercharged economy of Calgary, was busy.

But willing to put a different project on hold when he heard Jessica's situation, and that Jessica's furniture was currently residing on the lawn.

His attitude inspired confidence, and Kade found himself sharing the whole repair list with him. Jake promised to look at it first thing in the morning, even though it was Sunday, and get back to him with a cost estimate and a time frame.

"Can she stay out of the house for a couple of days? The floor sanding and refinishing causes a real mess. It's actually kind of a hazardous environment. Even the best floor sander can't contain all the dust, and it's full of chemicals. Plus it'll be easier for me to work if she's not there."

"Oh, sure," Kade said, thinking of Jessica staying here a few days. She probably wouldn't. She would probably insist on getting a hotel.

But for a little while longer, anyway, he was

still her husband. And he liked having her here, under his roof. He liked how protective he felt of her, and how he felt as if he could fix her world.

So he gave Jake the go-ahead.

As he disconnected his phone, Kade realized he needed to remember, when it came to larger issues, there was a lot he could not fix. This sense of having her under his protection was largely an illusion. They had tried it over the fire of real life, and they had been scorched.

Tomorrow, he would get up superearly and be gone before she even opened her eyes. He would solve all the helpless ambivalence she made him feel in the way he always had.

He would go to work.

He would, a little voice inside him said, abandon his wife. The same as always.

But it didn't quite work out that way. Because in the night, he was awakened to the sound of screaming.

Kade bolted from his bed and down the hall to her door. He paused outside it for a minute, aware, suddenly, he was in his underwear.

He heard a strangled sob, and the hesitation was over. He opened her door, and raced to her side. The bedside lamp was a touch lamp, and he brushed it with his hand.

Jessica was illuminated in the soft light. She was thrashing around, her hair a sweaty tangle, her eyes clenched tightly shut. When the light came on, she sat up abruptly, and the jolt to her arm woke her up.

She looked up at him, terrified, and then the terror melted into a look he could have lived for.

Had lived for, once upon a time, when he still believed in once upon a time.

"Are you okay?" he asked softly.

"Just a dream," she said, her voice hoarse.

He went into the adjoining bathroom and found a glass wrapped in plastic that crinkled when he stripped it off. Again, he was reminded this place was more like a hotel and not a home. He filled the glass and brought it to her.

She was sitting up now, with her back against the headboard, her eyes shut. "Sorry," she said.

"No, no, it's okay." He handed her the water. "How long have you been having the nightmares?"

"Since the break-in." She took a long drink of water. "I dream that someone is breaking into my house. My bedroom. That I wake up and—" She shuddered.

Kade felt a helpless anger at the burglar who had caused all this.

"Are you in your underwear?" she whispered.

"Yeah." He wanted to say it was nothing she had never seen before, but she looked suddenly shy, and it was adorable.

"You know I don't own a pair of pajamas," he reminded her.

He sat down on the bed beside her. Everything about her was adorable. She looked cute and very vulnerable in his too-large shirt with the buttons done up crooked. Her hair was sticking up on one side, and he had to resist the temptation to smooth it down with his hand. He noticed her eyes skittered everywhere but to his bare legs.

Sheesh. How long had they been married?

She seemed as if she might protest him getting in the bed, but instead, after a moment's thought, she scooted over, and he slid his legs up on the mattress beside her. He felt the soft familiar curve of her shoulder touching his, let the scent of her fill up his nose.

"I'm sorry about the nightmares," he said.

"It's silly," she said. "I think I'm getting post-traumatic stress disorder. It's shameful to get it for a very minor event."

"Hey, stop that. You were the victim here. The person who should be ashamed is whoever did this. Jessica, do these people not have any kind of conscience? Decency? Can they not know how these stupid things they do for piddling sums of money reverberate outward in a circle of pain and distress for their victims?"

He felt her relax, snuggle against him. "I feel sorry for him."

He snorted. "You would."

"I don't think you or I have ever known that kind of desperation, Kade."

Except that was not true. When she had wanted to have that baby, he had been desperate to make her happy. Desperate. And her own desperation had filled him with the most horrifying sense of helplessness.

He reached over and snapped off the light. His hand found her head, and he pulled it onto his shoulder, and stroked her hair.

"Go to sleep," he said softly. "I'll just stay with you until you do. You're safe. I'll take care of you. Why don't you lie back down."

"In a minute," she said huskily. "You know what this reminds me of, Kade?

"Hmm?"

"Remember when we first met, how I was terrified of thunderstorms?"

"Yeah," he said gruffly, "I remember."

"And then that one night, a huge electrical

storm was moving over the city, and you came and got me out of the bathroom where I was hiding."

"Under the sink," he recalled.

"And you led me outside, and you had the whole front step set up. You had a blanket out there, and a bottle of wine, and two glasses, and we sat on the step.

"At first I was terrified. I was quivering, I was so scared. I wanted to bolt. The clouds were so black. And the lightning was ripping open the heavens. I felt like Dorothy in the *Wizard of Oz*, as if I could be swept away.

"And then you put your hand on my shoulder, as if to hold me to the earth. You told me to count the seconds between the lightning bolt and the thunder hitting and I would know how far away the lightning strike was."

He remembered it all, especially her body trembling against his as the storm had intensified all around them.

"It kept getting closer and closer. Finally, there was no pause between the lightning strike and the thunder, there was not even time to count to one. The whole house shook. I could feel the rumble of the thunder ripple through you and through me and through the stairs and through the whole world. The tree in the front yard shook."

"Yeah, I remember."

"The whole night lit up in a flash, and I looked at you, and your face was illuminated by the lightning. You weren't even a little bit afraid. I could tell you loved it. You loved the fury and intensity of the storm. And suddenly, just like that, I wasn't afraid anymore. I loved it, too. Sitting out on the front steps with you, we sipped that wine, and cuddled under that blanket, and got soaked when the rain came."

She was silent for a long time.

"And after that," he said gently, "every time there was a storm, you were the first one out on that step."

"It's funny, isn't it? It cost nothing to go sit on those steps and storm watch. They came from nowhere. We couldn't plan it or expect it. And yet those moments?"

"I know, Jessica," he said softly. "The best. Those moments were the best."

"And today," she said, her voice slightly slurred with sleep, "today was a good day, like that."

"I nearly burned your house down."

"Our house," she corrected him. "You made me laugh. That made it worth it."

It made him realize how much pain was between them, and how much of it he had caused. He had a sense of wanting, somehow, to make it right between them. It bothered him, her casual admittance that she did not laugh much anymore. It bothered him, and he accepted responsibility for it.

So it could be a clean goodbye between him and Jessica. They could get a divorce without acrimony and without regret. So they could remember times like that, sitting in the thunderstorm, and know they had been made better for them. Not temporarily. But permanently.

He was a better man because of her.

CHAPTER THIRTEEN

PERHAPS, KADE THOUGHT, he was not the man he had wished to be or hoped to be, but still, he was better than he had been. Because of her, and because of the love they had shared.

Was there a way to honor that before they said goodbye? What if tomorrow, Sunday, he wasn't going to go to work after all?

Kade could tell something had shifted. Her head fell against his chest heavily, and he heard her breathing change.

And he knew he should get up and move, but there was something about this moment, this unexpected gift of his wife trusting him and being with him, that felt like one of those best moments ever, a moment just like sitting on the front step with her watching thunderstorms.

And so he accepted that he was reluctant to leave it. And eventually he fell asleep, sitting up, with Jessica's sweet weight nestled into him and the feel of the silk of her hair beneath his fingers.

Jessica woke to the most luxurious feeling of having slept well. The sun was spilling in her bedroom window. When she sat up and stretched, she saw that through the enormous windows of the bedroom, she had a view of the river and people jogging down the paths beside it.

Had she dreamed Kade had come into her room and they had talked about thunderstorms? It seemed as if she must have, because things had not been that easy between them for a long, long time.

And yet, when she looked, she was pretty sure the bedding beside her had been crushed from the weight of another person.

Far off in that big apartment, she heard a familiar sound.

Kade was whistling.

She realized she was surprised he was still here in the apartment. She glanced at the bedside clock. It was after nine. Sunday was just another workday for Kade. Usually he was in the office by seven. But not only was he here, he sounded happy.

Like the Kade of old.

There was a light tap on the door, and it swung open. Jessica pulled the covers up around her chin as if she was shy of him.

"I brought you a coffee."

She *was* shy of him. She realized she had not dreamed last night, because she had a sudden and rather mouthwatering picture of him in his underwear. Thankfully, he was fully dressed now, though he was still off the sexiness scale this morning.

It was obvious that Kade was fresh out of the shower, his dark hair towel roughened, a single beautiful bead of water sliding down his cheek to his jaw. Dressed in jeans, he had a thick white towel looped around his neck, and his chest and feet were deliciously bare.

She could look at that particular sight all day: the deepness of his chest, the chiseled perfection of his muscles, the ridged abs narrowing and disappearing into the waistband of jeans that hung low on slender hips. Her mouth actually went dry looking at him standing there.

He came in and handed her the coffee. It smelled wonderful—though not as wonderful as his fresh-from-the-shower scent—and she reached out for it. Their fingers touched, and the intensity sizzled in the air between them.

She knew that no part of last night had been a dream. He had slipped onto the bed beside her, and they had talked of thunderstorms, and she had fallen asleep with his big shoulder under her head.

She took a steadying sip of the coffee. It was one of those unexpectedly perfect moments. Kade had always made the best coffee. He delighted in good coffee and was always experimenting with different beans, which he ground himself. It had just the right amount of cream and no sugar.

He remembered. Silly to feel so wonderful that he remembered how she liked her coffee. The luxury of the bed, the sun spilling in the window, the coffee, him delivering it bare chested—yes, an unexpectedly perfect moment.

"I just talked to Jake," he said, taking a sip of his own coffee, and eyeing her over the rim of it.

"Who?"

"Jake. The contractor who fixed the door at your shop. He's over at your house."

"He's at my house at, what is it, seven o'clock on Sunday morning? How do you get a contractor, especially a good one, to do that?"

"I used my substantial charm."

"And your substantial checkbook?" she asked sweetly.

He pretended to be offended. "He's going to do the list of all the things that need fixing—the leak in the roof and the toilet handle and the floors, which really need refinishing now. And he'll fix the new smoke damage on the ceiling, too. That's the good news."

"Uh-oh, there's bad news."

"Yeah. There always is, isn't there? It's going to take him the better part of a week to get everything done. And he says it will go a lot smoother if you aren't there."

She concentrated hard on her coffee. "Oh," she finally squeaked out. A week of this? Coffee delivered by a gorgeous man whom she happened to know intimately? Who had joined her last night in bed in his underwear? She'd be a basket case. "Look, obviously I can't stay here. I'll call a friend. Or get a hotel."

"Why is it obvious you can't stay here?" he asked.

"Kade, we're getting a divorce. We're supposed to be fighting, not setting up as roommates." Certainly she should not be feeling this way about the near nudity of a man she was about to divorce!

"'From where the sun now stands, I will fight no more forever,'" he said softly.

"I hate it when you quote Chief Joseph." No, she didn't. She loved it. She loved it as much as she loved that he had made her coffee exactly as she liked it, without even having to ask.

She loved that he remembered she had once bought a piece of art—that they couldn't afford—with a part of that quote as its name. She remembered that he hadn't been mad. He'd turned the piece over in his hands—a shard of gourd, burned with an Appaloosa galloping across it toward the sun—and he'd smiled and said, "Worth starving for a few weeks."

And, of course, they hadn't starved.

But of course, that had been at the beginning, when her staying home and having a house of her own and a husband to look after had been so novel. Later, it seemed as if Kade was nothing but annoyed when she bought things for the house. She thought of reminding him of that.

But it seemed too petty. She slid him a look now. Was he quoting that because they were turning over a new leaf? Because they were not going to squabble anymore?

Everybody squabbled when they got divorced.

"You want to do something fun today?" he

asked. "Since fixing the house has been removed from our list?"

No, she did not want to do something fun! She wanted to get a divorce. She wanted to sell the house they had shared. She wanted to cut ties with him. She wanted to adopt a baby and get on with her life, without him. Fun? Who had fun in the middle of a divorce?

"I thought I took the fun out of everything," she said. She put the coffee down and folded her arms over the largeness of his shirt, which she suddenly wished was at least a little sexy. She recognized the treachery of her thoughts.

He looked bewildered. "You took the fun out of everything?"

"That's what you said. The day you left."

Kade looked genuinely shocked. "I didn't say that."

"Yes, you did." The words, in fact, felt burned into her, as if they had become part of who she was.

"Are you sure?"

"Oh, yeah."

He looked genuinely distressed, but she found she couldn't let it go.

"So," she said, trying for a bright, light note, "what do you do for fun? You're probably an expert at it, now that the dead weight isn't around your neck anymore."

"Jessica, I don't remember saying that. It must have been one of those mean, in-the-heat-of-the-moment things. I'm sorry."

She shrugged, as if it didn't matter one little bit, as if she had not mulled over those words every single day for a year.

"So if we *were* going to do something fun today—and I'm not saying that we are—what would you suggest?" Did it sound as if she was forgiving him? *Was* she forgiving him? "Remember, I have one arm out of commission. Skydiving is out. Ditto for rock climbing. And bull riding."

"I said that? That you took the fun out of everything?"

"Yes! And then you packed your bag, and you left, and you never looked back."

"I thought you'd call, Jessica."

"Why would I call? You were the one who left." She hesitated. She tried to strip any hurt from her voice. "I thought you'd call."

"I didn't know what to say."

"Neither did I. I wasn't going to beg you to come back."

"Why would you beg me to come back?" he asked wearily. "And I guess that's why I didn't call, either. We had reached a complete impasse. We were utterly and exhaustingly miserable. We just seemed to go in endless circles. You wanted a baby. I'd had enough."

She could see the very real pain in his face. For the first time? Had she really been so wrapped up in herself and what she wanted that she could not see what it was doing to him? She'd accused him of being insensitive to her, but she saw now it had been a two-way street. She felt an odd little shiver of awareness go up her spine.

"So," Jessica said carefully, trying to navigate the minefield between them without getting blown up, "answer the question. What do you do with a one-armed woman for fun?"

His eyes fastened on her lips.

"Stop it," she said.

"Stop what?" he asked innocently.

"Looking at me like that. I think *that* would be quite a challenge one armed."

"What?" he asked innocently.

"You know."

He smiled wickedly. "I think *that* could be quite a lot of fun.

"I think it would be darn near impossible."

"I don't. I like a challenge. I like figuring things out."

Good grief, she could not stay here for days with this kind of delicious sensual tension in the air between them.

"I could start by offering to help you shower," he said, his voice a low growl.

She threw the pillow at him. It was a clean miss, but he dodged anyway, managing to save his coffee. He laughed and made a face at her. "So are we agreed? We'll do something fun today?"

"I suppose, if you promise to be good," she said warningly, reaching for the other pillow.

"Do I have to? Okay, okay." And then he backed away from her, closed the door and was gone.

She freshened up in the bathroom and put on the maternity dress. When she saw her reflection in the full-length mirror of his opulent guest bathroom, she felt she had succeeded just a little too well in her goals.

She had wanted to look as if she didn't care! She was not sure she had wanted to look quite this bad! She looked like a waif abandoned outside an orphanage. Still, defiantly, refusing to give in to the temptation to win his approval in any way, least of all by trying to make herself attractive to him, she stepped out of the bathroom.

The truth was she hadn't brought anything else anyway. She had thought her stay here was going to be brief. Given the shakiness of her resolve, looking pathetic seemed as if it could only be a good thing.

He was behind the kitchen counter putting croissants—obviously freshly delivered—on a plate.

"Wow. Excuse me while I pluck out my eyes. I'd forgotten the full ugliness of that dress. Or maybe I blocked it. Trauma."

"It is not that bad." He still had not put on a shirt. In the "life was unfair" department, this seemed to rate quite high: that he wanted to pluck out his eyes and she wanted to gaze at him endlessly.

"It is. That bad. Believe me. At least its awfulness helps me figure out the agenda for the day. We need to go shopping first."

"I am not going shopping. I love this dress." She didn't actually. She thought it was quite hideous. "I'm sorry you'll be embarrassed by me, but that's the way it is."

"I'm not embarrassed by you. But in the 'find something to be grateful for' department—"

She squinted at him suspiciously. He was not a "find something to be grateful for" kind of guy.

"I'm just glad you didn't bring the camo one. If we end up in the woods today, I don't want to misplace you."

"What are the chances we'll end up in the woods?"

"Anything can happen when you just let the day unfold."

She should not feel nearly as thrilled by that as she did! But spontaneity had not been part of her world for a long time, and Jessica suddenly felt eager for it.

CHAPTER FOURTEEN

ONE THING THAT Jessica remembered about Kade with complete fondness was that he always seemed open to what the world could bring him.

They had a simple breakfast at his apartment. He had had the still-steaming croissants and preserves delivered, and they sat out on the terrace and ate in the new warmth of the spring light. What was it about spring that brought hope to even the most wounded heart?

He seemed to forget she looked ugly. She seemed to forget he looked gorgeous. The old comfort rose up between them.

They talked as if nothing had ever gone wrong between them. It was like the old days, when spending time with him felt as if she was spending time with her best friend. The conversation flowed easily and naturally, words spilling out of them, as if they were anxious to catch up. They talked about mutual friends, his aunt Helen and her cousin Dave. They talked a bit about their businesses.

And then they left his place and walked downtown. Jessica became self-consciously aware of the ugliness of her dress again as she walked beside him. Kade was dressed casually in a sports shirt and summer khaki pants, and yet she could not help but notice how he got *that* look from women. Interested. Admiring. Hungry for a taste of that particular delight. They would glance at her, too, and then dismiss her.

When he came around to her good arm and his hand found hers, her own sense of hunger deepened. She was so aware of how much she had missed this, the small intimacies that made a relationship, the feel of his hand, strong, closing possessively around her own, sending that message to all who passed: *taken*.

She was determined to make a go of it on her own, but that simple thing, him taking her hand, filled her with a longing that felt physical in its intensity, like a shiver going up and down her spine that would not go away.

If she was smart, she would drop his hand and turn and run.

But smart seemed to have abandoned her. She wanted these moments. It felt as if she was stealing them to store away, as a part of her, for when she did not have him anymore. She actually felt thankful that *these* memories might overlay the old ones. Their history, leading up to the separation, was so filled with bitterness and anger and frustration that it had become as if the dark colors of a new painting had completely obliterated the light of the old painting that existed right underneath it.

They entered the downtown. It was a beautiful day so they avoided the Plus 15 Skywalk and instead strolled the pedestrian mall on Stephen Avenue. Downtown did not have its weekday bustle, the throngs of men and women in business attire, but there was still a colorful conglomeration of shoppers and activities on the streets.

A cowboy-hatted busker had set up close to Stephen Avenue Walk and was singing lustily. They stopped and watched for a few minutes. Kade dropped a five into his guitar case and they moved on.

They enjoyed the historic sandstone buildings of one of Canada's few designated National Historic Sites. Calgarians had been conducting their commerce here on Eighth Avenue for over a hundred years. They passed the building where Kade worked, in the heart of Calgary's financial district, and then walked along the column-fronted arcade of the very impressive Hudson's Bay Company building. The building had always anchored Calgary's downtown core.

"How about there?"

She looked at the store Kade had paused to point out. It was a tiny but very upscale boutique called Chrysalis, which Jessica knew of but had never set foot in. "I can't go in there."

"Why?"

Mostly because of how she was dressed right now! "I can't afford anything in there."

"I can."

"No."

"Come on. It will be fun. Remember that scene we liked in that movie?"

"Pretty Woman?" she guessed.

He nodded happily. "Let's reenact that."

"I'm no Julia Roberts," she said, but she could feel herself being drawn into his playfulness. Where had all the playfulness gone between them?

"You are way better than her," he said, and he looked at her with such genuine male appreciation that she nearly melted.

They went into the shop. It was understated and tasteful. But the salesclerk was a very chic young woman with an outrageous purple streak in her blond hair. She rushed at them, probably, Jessica thought, to get rid of her, the same as in the movie.

"My first customers of the day," she said gleefully. Then she eyed Jessica with the look of a seasoned fashion aficionado. Rather than judgment or snobbery, Jessica sensed friendliness and very genuine concern. "What is that you are wearing?"

In a tone that should be reserved for "I'm so sorry to hear about the death in your family."

"I'm having a little trouble with my arm," Jessica said defensively.

"Even so, you're lovely! And just a little bit of a thing. You have to show off your assets!" She cast Kade a look that clearly said, "Especially if you are with a guy who looks like that," and that she clearly considered him an asset worth keeping.

"Thank you. We'll just have a quick look around," Jessica said.

"No, no, *no*. I am going to guide you through your Chrysalis experience."

"Oh, dear," Jessica mumbled, and sent Kade a pleading look. *Get me out of here*. But Kade folded his arms over his chest and shrugged slightly. *Let's just go with it*.

"I will have you fixed up in no time. In fact,

I will love working with you. Caterpillar to butterfly, as our name suggests. I'm Holly, by the way."

The girl's enthusiasm was so genuine that Jessica could not even stir herself to annoyance at being called, basically, an insect pupa.

"Usually, I would ask about your lifestyle, but today I think you're looking for some things that are easier to get in and out of, aren't you?"

Kade frowned at Holly. "We were hoping for someone more like the salesclerk in *Pretty Woman*. You know? If you could just be snotty, and then I flash my gold card at you and you fall all over yourself trying to help us out."

Holly laughed. "Well, I like the gold card part. And I always fall all over myself trying to help people out." She looked at Jessica. "How would you feel if I just put you in a change room and found some things that I think would work for you?"

Jessica should be insulted. She was obviously being told she could not be trusted to pick out her own things, but given the dress she had on, could she blame the girl?

"I like to encourage everyone to let me pick some things for them," Holly said. "You know, people get in shopping ruts."

Out of the corner of her vision, Jessica saw

Kade roll his eyes at the near religious fervor Holly apparently had for the shopping experience.

Undaunted, Holly went on. "They pick variations of the same thing for themselves over and over. Sometimes a fresh eye can be amazing. And then, you can model what I pick out for you for your extremely handsome boyfriend."

"Husband," Kade said. "Though I like the handsome part."

"Oh, sorry. No rings," Holly said. She squinted at him. "Though you look as though you've had one on recently."

Jessica's gaze flew to Kade's ring finger. Sure enough, a white band of skin marked where his wedding ring had been. The band had been there recently, obviously, since such marks faded rather quickly. What did it mean that he had worn his ring so recently?

Stay in the moment, she ordered herself sternly. She had one mission today. To have fun. To let go. To be free. And if she ended up, with Holly's help, looking a little bit better than she looked right now, she'd go with that, too.

For once, Jessica felt no desire at all to hide behind their upcoming divorce.

She followed Holly obediently to the back of the store. There was a classy sitting area there for Kade, complete with a comfy deep upholstered chair and a huge flat-screen TV. Holly handed him the remote, and then shooed Jessica into an opulent change room.

Minutes later, she was back. "I don't mean to be presumptuous, but I brought you this." She held up a bra. "Front closing."

And sexy as all get out. Jessica took the bra with her good hand and suddenly ached to put it on. To give herself permission to be feminine and beautiful.

She had not felt like a beautiful woman since her husband had left her. Despite career success, somehow she carried loneliness and defeat within her.

A thought, unwelcome, came out of nowhere.

Had she been planning on using a child to combat her pervasive feeling of inadequacy? She shook off the shadow that passed over her. Today was just about fun. She had given herself over to introspection quite enough in the past year.

"You are a lifesaver," Jessica told Holly, and then surrendered to the process. She allowed herself to be spoiled completely. Holly did have an exceptional eye for fashion, and along with the bra, she had soon provided Jessica with a stack of clothing topped by a filmy jade silk top.

None of it was anything Jessica would have chosen for herself. She had become the master of understated. Almost all her clothes were in neutrals, grays and taupes, as if, she realized with a start, she was trying to make herself invisible.

Jessica fingered the silk and felt a pure and simple longing. To be pretty.

It occurred to her she had not cared about being pretty since long before Kade had left her. Since she had lost the second baby.

"This will be amazing with your eyes. And look—Velcro fasteners!"

"You found a top with a Velcro closure? Is this really silk? Where's the price tag?"

"Your Prince Charming out there told me to take the price tags off."

"Humph," she said, but she didn't feel nearly as annoyed as she should have. She didn't have to buy it, she reminded herself. She just had to have fun with it.

Soon, the ensemble was completed with an easy-to-pull-on skirt with a flirty hemline and a delicate pair of sandals that Jessica could just slip her feet into.

"You look awesome," Holly said. "Go show him."

Jessica stared at herself in the mirror. "Um,

I think I look a bit too young." Plus, the blouse was extremely sheer, which explained Holly bringing a sexy bra with it.

"Nonsense."

"This looks like something a teenager would wear. Don't you think the skirt is a little, um, short? Not to mention the blouse is a little, er, see-through."

"When you have legs like that? Show them off, girlfriend. Same with your other assets. Now go show him! He'll let you know how right that look is for you."

Feeling strangely shy about sharing this oddly intimate moment with Kade, the same as she had felt this morning sharing space with him, Jessica exited the change room. Kade had found a football game on TV and didn't even look impatient. He looked content.

And then he noticed her. He flipped off the sound. His eyes darkened. She suddenly didn't care how short the skirt was or if the blouse was see-through. She did a saucy little spin.

"Wow," he said, his voice hoarse. "You look incredible. Two thumbs-up to that one."

Jessica didn't just feel beautiful for the first time in a long time. She felt sexy. It felt unbelievably good to feel sexy with no agenda, no calendar lurking in the back of her mind, no temperature to take. It felt, well, fun. And after that, she just gave herself over to the experience completely.

It was fun, having Holly help her in and out of outfits, and then modeling them for Kade, who was a great audience. He raised his eyebrows, and did low wolf whistles and louder ones. He made her feel as if she was not only sexy and beautiful, but as if she was the only woman in the world he felt that way about.

But even so, Jessica had to draw the line somewhere, and she drew it at an evening dress Holly hauled in.

"I have absolutely nowhere to wear such a thing," she said. Still, she touched it wistfully. Like everything in Chrysalis, the cut and the fabric were mouthwatering. "I won't be able to get it on over my arm."

"Sure you will," Holly said. "It's back fastening, so I'll just drop it over your head, like this, and poof. Ooh, butterfly."

It took a bit more work for them to get her arm out the sleeve, but then she was standing there looking at herself, stunned.

Her hair was flyaway from all the in-and-out of trying on clothes, but somehow that added to the sense of electricity in the air. The dress, the color of licking flame, fit her like a glove, then flared out at the bottom in a mermaid hemline.

"Here." Holly crouched at her feet. "Let me slip these on you."

As if in a dream, Jessica lifted one foot and then the other. She stared at herself in the mirror. The heels had added three inches to her height. The cast and sling on her arm might as well have disappeared, the outfit was so attention grabbing, especially with a very deep, plunging neckline.

Holly stood back and looked at her with satisfaction. "*This* is exactly what I envisioned from the moment you walked through the door. Go show him."

Should she? What was the point? It didn't feel fun anymore. It felt strangely intense, almost like the moment she had walked toward him down that long aisle in her wedding dress.

She was going to protest, but when Holly held open the door for her, Jessica sucked in her breath and walked out. Holly slid away.

Kade didn't look right away. "Don't drop it!" he yelled at the TV. And then he turned and saw her. Without taking his eyes off her, he turned off the remote. The television screen went blank. He stood up. His mouth fell open and then he shut it, and rocked back on his heels, looking at her with eyes narrowed with passion.

This was what she had missed when that moment she had glided down the aisle toward him had been replaced by the pressures of everyday living, by disappointments, by hurts, by misunderstandings.

"Jessie," he whispered.

This was what she had missed. She leaned toward him.

CHAPTER FIFTEEN

JESSIE LEANED TOWARD HIM, looking at him with heavy-lidded eyes.

Pretty woman...walking down the street... The music seemed to explode into the small dressing room and waiting area. Jessica gasped and put her hand to her throat, wobbled on the high heels.

Kade was in front of her instantly, looking down at her with concern.

"Sorry," she said. "I keep startling from loud noises."

He cocked his head at her. The room flooded with Roy Orbison's distinctive vocals. Kade took one step closer to her. He held out his hand, and she didn't hesitate, not for one second. She took his hand. Kade drew her to him and rocked her against him.

And then, as if they had planned it, as if they had never stopped dancing with each other, they were moving together. Even though the tempo of the song was fast, they did not dance that way.

They slow danced around the waiting area, their bodies clinging to each other, their gazes locked. The music faded, but they didn't let go, but stood very still, drinking each other in, as if they could make up for a whole year lost.

Holly burst in. "How cool was that, that I found—" She stopped. "Whoa. You two are *hot*."

Kade's arms slid away from Jessica. He stepped back. He swept a hand through his hair. "We'll take it," he said.

"That dress?" Holly said.

"No. Everything. Every single thing she tried on."

Jessica's mouth opened, but the protest was stuck somewhere in her throat, and not a single sound came out. She turned and went back into the change cubicle.

"Wear this one," Holly suggested, following her in. She dug through the pile of clothing to the very first outfit Jessica had tired on, the jade top and skirt.

But she didn't want to wear that one. Her world felt totally rattled by what had just happened, by how spontaneously she and Kade had gone into each other's arms. She wanted to feel safe again.

"Where's the dress I came in here with?"

Holly giggled. "He told me to throw it away."

"What?"

"Yeah, he said to grab it at my first opportunity and dispose of it."

"And you just listened to him? That's outrageous."

"He's very masterful," Holly said with an unapologetic sigh. "Besides—" she winked "—he's the one with the credit card."

Jessica thought of the frank male appreciation in his eyes as she had modeled her new outfits, and she contemplated how she was feeling right now.

Alive. One hundred percent in the land of the living, the life force tingling along the surface of her skin. Did she really want to go back to safety? To reclaim that familiar wooden feeling she had lived with for so long?

Why not, just for today, embrace this? That she was alive? And that her life was alight with the unexpected element of fun? And with the unexpected sizzle of attraction between her and the man she had married.

They left the store with Kade's arms loaded with parcels, and with her feeling fresh and flirty and like a breath of spring in the first out-fit she had tried on. He had paid for everything.

"I'll pay you back," she said. He had insisted on buying every single thing she had donned, even the evening gown.

Since the theme of the day was fun, she'd given in. But buying the gown? That was just silly. She had nowhere to wear an evening gown. Her future plans did not involve any-thing that would require formal wear. In fact, she needed to be stocking up on comfy pants and sweatshirts that could hold up to baby puke and other fluids associated with the delights of motherhood.

But she had been so caught up in the mo-ment, and the dress had made her feel so un-characteristically glamorous—sexy, even—that she had actually wanted to be silly. She had wanted to purchase that piece of silk and gossa-mer that had made her feel better than a movie star.

She should have protested more—she knew that when the bill was totaled—but the look in his eyes when he had seen her had sold every single outfit to her. She'd had a ridiculous sense of *needing* those clothes, though in her heart, she knew what she wanted was the look in his eyes. "Once we sell the house, I'll pay you back," she said firmly.

"Whatever. Hey, this stuff is already heavy. Look. There's one of those rickshaw things being pulled by a bike. Have you ever been in one of those?"

"No."

He juggled the packages to his left arm, put his two fingers to his lips and let out a piercing whistle. The driver, a fit-looking twentysomething guy, pulled over.

"Where to?"

"Ah, we aren't sure yet. I think we need you for the day. Have you got a day rate?"

"I do now!"

Jessica knew she should have protested when the driver named his rate, but somehow she just couldn't. She and Kade piled into the narrow seat of the rickshaw, squished together, all their packages bunched in with them.

"Where to?"

"We need a picnic lunch," Kade decided. "And a bottle of wine. And a forest. Maybe Yan's for the lunch. Do you feel like Szechuan?"

She thought of all those menus she had sorted through yesterday, each one representing a memory. She loved Szechuan-style Chinese food. "Two orders of ginger beef," she reminded him.

Their driver took off across the downtown, darting in and out of traffic, getting them honked at, shaking his fist and yelling obscenities at drivers of vehicles.

It was hysterically funny, and she could not stop laughing. That wondrous feeling of being alive continued to tingle along the surface of her skin.

"You're going to get us killed," she said with a laugh as a cab they had cut off laid on the horn. She clung to Kade's arm as the rickshaw swayed violently, and then their driver bumped up on a curb. "Or get my other arm broken."

He twirled an imaginary moustache. "Ah, getting you right where I want you. Helpless. And then I can ply my lethal charms against you."

Kade flopped down on the blanket that he had purchased. The driver had found them a quiet spot on Prince's Island, and had managed to make himself scarce while Kade and Jessica enjoyed their picnic under a leafy tree, with the sound of the river in the background. Now, after too much food, and most of a bottle of wine, Kade felt sleepy and relaxed.

"Two orders of ginger beef," he moaned. "It's masochistic."

"Nobody was forcing you to eat it."

"You know why we always have to buy two, though." *Always*, as if there was not a yearlong blank spot in their relationship, as if they could just pick up where they had left off. He considered where they had left off, and thought, despite his current level of comfort with Jessica, why would they want to?

"Yes, we always have to buy two because you eat the first one by yourself, and most of the second one."

"Guilty," he moaned. "My tummy hurts, Jessie."

"And three spring rolls," she reminded him. "And most of the sizzling rice." Despite the sternness in her tone, when he opened one eye, she was smiling. She looked as utterly content as he could remember her looking in a long, long time.

He lifted up his shirt and showed her his tummy. She sighed, and scooted over beside him, that teeny-tiny skirt hitching way up her legs, and rubbed his stomach with gentle hands.

"Ah," he said, and closed his eyes. Maybe it was because he had not slept well last night, or maybe it was because he had eaten too much, or maybe it was because his world felt right for the first time in over a year, but with a sigh of contentment, he went to sleep.

When he woke up, she was sleeping curled up beside him. He slid his arm around her shoulders and pulled her into his side, being careful of her arm.

"Did we fall asleep?" she asked.

"Yeah."

"Is our driver still here? Or did he take off with all my new stuff?"

Kade got up on one elbow. He could see the rickshaw over by the riverbank. When he craned his head, he could see the driver tapping earnestly at his phone with his thumbs.

"I haven't paid him yet. He's not going anywhere." He slid his own phone out of his pocket and checked the time. "Holy, it's four o'clock already."

"It's been a perfect day," she said.

"Agreed. What was the best part for you? The shopping? I love the long dress."

"I don't have a single place to wear a dress like that," she said. "I shouldn't have bought it."

"Yes, you should have. I want you to accept it as a gift from me. You can pay me back for the rest of that stuff if you insist—"

"Which I do!"

"But I want to buy that dress."

"Why do you want to buy me a dress that I probably will never wear?"

"Wear it around the house. Put a movie on, and wear it to watch it. Eat popcorn in it."

She laughed. "That seems eccentric and foolhardy. What if I got butter on it?"

"That's what I liked about it. You know what it reminded me of, Jess?"

"No. What?" She held her breath.

"It reminded me of those paintings you used to do, the ones that were all swirling colors and amazing motion."

"I haven't thought about those for years," she said.

"Save the dress and wear it to the unveiling of your first art show."

She laughed a little nervously. "I'm not having a first art show."

"But that's what I've always wondered. Where did that part of you go?"

"I paint murals," she said. "That's my creative outlet."

"I don't think bunnies on walls do justice to your gifts," he said.

"I don't care what you think!" she snapped. "Sorry. Let's not ruin the moment with you telling me how to live my life."

She was right. This was not any of his business, not anymore. Maybe it never had been.

"Is there any ginger beef left?" he asked wistfully.

"No."

"How about sizzling rice?"

And then the moment of tension was gone, and she laughed and passed him the container. It seemed like the most natural thing in the world to go home to his place together. And then to say good-night with unnatural formality and to go to their separate bedrooms.

The next morning, they both got up. He ordered croissants again. She came out to eat one in the too-large shirt.

"I guess I should have been shopping for pajamas instead of evening dresses," she said.

What kind of kettle of worms would it open up, he wondered, if he said he liked what she had on—his shirt—way better than pajamas?

"Are you coming back here after you've finished work?" he asked her. He was holding his breath waiting for her reply.

"I guess," she said, and he heard in her voice the very same things he was feeling. What were they reopening, exactly, by living under the same roof? What were they moving toward? Were they putting a framework in place for their future relationship? Was it possible they could be one of those rare amicably divorced couples who were friends?

He hoped things would become clear in the next few days, because he did not like uncertainty. And at the moment, his future seemed murky, like looking into a most uncooperative crystal ball.

CHAPTER SIXTEEN

MONDAY, AFTER WORK, Jessica returned to Kade's apartment. She was somewhat ashamed that she had not done a single thing to make new living arrangements for herself. And now here she was, aware she was waiting for the door of the apartment to open.

Why? Kade never came home at regular hours. What was she waiting for? Hadn't this been part of their whole problem? That she waited, as if her whole life depended on him, and he had a whole life that had nothing to do with her?

Surely she'd come further than this, still waiting for him to come home! It was pathetic, and she was not being pathetic anymore. And so, instead of sitting in the apartment, she went and explored his building.

There was a good-size pool that they were conducting a kayaking class in, and beside that was a climbing wall. She went and sat on a bench and watched people climb the wall.

A good-looking man came over and introduced himself as Dave and asked her if she was going to try it.

She held up her arm. "Already did," she said, deadpan. He laughed and flirted with her a bit, and she realized whatever had happened when she had put on all those clothes had been good. She was wearing one of her new outfits, and it seemed to fill her with confidence she hadn't had for some time. Dave went up the wall, obviously showing off, and she was content to let him.

She watched for a while, and decided as soon as her arm got better, she would try climbing. The wall looked really fun.

After doing a thorough tour of the building and the gorgeous gardens outside, which included that impressive waterfall at the front, she wandered back to the apartments.

Kade was there. Did he look pleased when she let herself in using the code he had given her?

"Hey," he said. "How was your day?"

"Oh, I struggled through."

"Work late?"

"Oh, no, I've been back for a while. I thought

I'd check out your building. It's great. I love the climbing wall."

"Really? I've never been on it. Is that one of the outfits we bought yesterday?"

"Yeah, I've had lots of comments on it. A guy named Dave, down at the climbing wall, stopped to talk to me. I don't think he normally would have mistaken me for his type."

She felt just the littlest thrill of pleasure that Kade could not hide his annoyance at Dave's attention.

"Want to order something for dinner? I don't have much here to cook." He snapped his fingers. "Unless you want an omelet."

He'd always made the best omelets.

"Perfect," she said.

And it was perfect. After dinner they watched the news together, and it felt so utterly easy, as if they were an old married couple.

Which they were, sort of.

Of course, when they'd been a newly married couple, they hadn't sat around watching television. They couldn't keep their hands off each other. Later, when that stage had passed— or when she'd killed it, by bringing out the dreaded chart—they had played cards sometimes in the evening.

She suddenly longed for that.

"You have a deck of cards, Kade?"

"Why? You want to play strip poker?" he asked with such earnest hopefulness she burst out laughing.

"No!"

"How about a strip Scrabble game, then?"

"How about just an ordinary Scrabble game?" she said, trying not to encourage him by laughing.

"Can we use bad words?"

"I suppose that would be okay. Just this once."

"How about if we use only bad words?"

She gave him a slug on his arm. "That falls into the 'give him an inch and he'll take a mile' category."

Suddenly, she wanted to play a bad-words Scrabble game with him. She wanted to not be the uptight one, the stick-in-the-mud. "A bad-words Scrabble game it is," she said.

"I don't actually have a Scrabble board."

"That figures."

"But I bet we can find it on the computer."

And so that was what they did, sat side by side on his sofa, playing a bad-words Scrabble game on the computer until she was laughing so hard it felt as if she could die from it.

"So," he said casually, after he had just

played *phaut,* "tell me why you want a divorce all of a sudden."

"I told you, it's not all of a sudden."

"But there's something going on."

And, maybe he'd done this on purpose, reminded her of what it was like to have a best friend, because she wanted to tell him. Crazily, she wanted to know what he thought.

"I'm thinking of adopting a baby," she said quietly.

He was staring at her. "Aw, Jess," he said, not as if he was happy for her, but as if he pitied her.

"What does that mean?" she asked.

"It's the Old English spelling of *fart,*" he said. "*P-h-a-u-t.* You can challenge it if you want. But you miss a turn if you're wrong."

She had just told him something very important! How could he act as if the stupid word he'd made up was more engrossing?

"Not *that.* What does 'aw, Jess' mean?"

"Never mind. I'm sorry I said it."

She saw, suddenly, that he was using his stupid made-up word as a way not to get into it with her. "No, I want you to tell me."

"But then when I do, you'll be mad," he said, confirming his avoidance strategy.

"Will I?" When had she become that person? The one who invited opinions, but then was angry if they were not what she wanted to hear? She wanted it not to be a truth about her, but in her gut, she knew it was.

"You don't want to hear what I have to say, but maybe I'm going to say it anyway, for the sake of the baby."

She felt as if she was bracing herself.

"A baby isn't supposed to fill a need in you, Jessica," he said quietly. "You're supposed to fulfill its needs."

Jessica felt the shock of it. She felt as if she should be very, very angry with him. But she was not. Instead, she remembered the revelation she'd had in the change room of Chrysalis, the one she had tried to shake off.

That she was using a child to try to fight off her own pervasive feeling of inadequacy. Instead of being angry with Kade, Jessica was, instead, sharply aware she had carried a certain neediness in her since the death of her mother. The miscarriages had made it worse.

So Kade had called a spade a spade. She saw, from the look on his face, it was not a put-down at all. She had a deep sense of his courage, that he had handed her a simple truth, knowing it might make her angry, but also believing she needed to hear it. And maybe also believing she would know what to do with it.

Jessica remembered how before she had hated everything about Kade, she had loved everything about him. And this was one of the things she had loved, that he had a way of seeing right to the heart of things. He would have shrugged it off, uncomfortable, if she called it intuition, but that was exactly what it was.

It was part of what made him so good at business. He was brilliantly insightful. Before things had gone sideways between them, Jessica had loved his input, so different from her own.

"I've been too blunt," he said. "I'm sorry."

"No, Kade," she said, "it's what I needed to hear, even if it's not what I wanted to hear."

She suspected this was why she had not wanted to tell him about the adoption, because he could shed a light on her plans that could change everything.

"You and I," she said, "we've always been so different. It's as if we each have the pieces of half of a puzzle. It's when we're together that we can piece together the whole thing."

She thought of those adoption papers at home, and it occurred to her this was what he had shown her: she was still wanting a baby to fill gaps in her life.

She had probably never been less ready for a baby than she was right now.

"I'm very tired now," she whispered, feeling as if she was holding the remnants of another shattered dream within herself. "I'm going to bed."

"Jess, I'm sorry. I didn't want to hurt you."

She smiled wanly. "Oh, Kade, I don't think we ever wanted to hurt each other. And yet, somehow we always do."

And yet, over the next few days it was as if something had broken free between them; a wall of ice had crumbled, and what was held behind it flowed out. As they shared his beautiful space, there were moments of spontaneous laughter. And quiet companionship. As they shared meals and memories and old connections, they rediscovered their comfort with one another. And caught glimpses of the joy they had once shared. And relaxed into that rare sensation of having found someone in the world with whom it was possible to be genuine.

And so when Jake called Kade on Thursday afternoon and told him that the house was done, Kade felt not happy that the work had been finished so quickly, but a sense of loss. He wanted to give Jake a list of ten more things to do. No, a hundred. No, a thousand.

He brought her the news after work. Jessica had arrived at the apartment before him. She was wearing one of the outfits they had bought together—a lively floral-print dress with a belt and a wide skirt that reminded him of something someone might wear to dance the jive.

She had her arm out of the sling and was wiping down his counters. Once it had bugged him so much that she felt driven to wipe up every crumb.

But now, watching her, he could see it gave her a kind of contentment to be bringing order to her space, and he found he liked watching her.

She looked up and saw him standing there, and she smiled a greeting.

"Hey! You are not supposed to be out of that sling yet."

"You know me."

It was the most casual of statements, but it filled him with some sense of satisfaction that, yes, he did know her.

"I could not handle the mess on the counter. I needed both hands free to wring out the dish-cloth."

"You've always been such a stickler for tidy."

"I know. You used to protest daily, *too many rules.*"

"Did I? I don't remember that."

Jessica cast Kade a look. Could he really not remember the mean things he had said to her?

"You called me the sock Nazi," she remembered ruefully. Was she hoping he would apologize? He didn't. He cocked his head at her, and looked at her in that way that made her stomach do the roller-coaster thing.

"I couldn't understand the changes in you," he said. "We said 'I do' and overnight you went from being this kind of Bohemian free-spirited artist to Martha Stewart's understudy."

"And you," she reminded him, "resisted me at every turn. It drove me crazy. If I put out a laundry hamper, you would throw your dirty clothes on the floor beside it."

It had driven her crazy that she had been creating this perfect little nest for them—a perfect world, really—and he'd resisted her at every turn. He'd left his socks in the living room. He'd hung his towels crooked in the bathroom. He'd left dishes in the sink, and if he'd been working outside and forgot something in the house, he'd just traipsed in, leaving a pathway of leaves and grass and mud in his wake.

"I know I could be inconsiderate," he said, but he didn't sound very remorseful. "I felt as if you were trying to control me all the time, I felt as if you thought the way you wanted to live was the only correct way, and what I wanted, to be a little relaxed in my own space, didn't count at all."

Jessica felt shocked by that. It was certainly true. She had always wanted things her way.

"And then I'd come home from working all day, and you'd have some elaborate meal all prepared and candles on the table and the best dishes out. I would have been just as happy with a hamburger and my feet up on the coffee table in front of the TV. Not that I was allowed to put my feet up on the coffee table, even though it was really a bench that was sturdy enough to have survived one war, a fire and two floods."

She was aghast at the picture he was painting. He looked as if he was going to stop, but now that the floodgates were open, he was completely unable to.

"I wanted to talk to you the way we had always talked—about ideas and dreams and your art. I wanted to laugh with you and be lighthearted.

"But suddenly all you wanted to talk about was paint colors for the nursery and could we please get a new sofa, and did I think there was too much tarragon in the recipe. *Tarragon*, Jess."

And so this was how their relationship had started to show cracks, she thought. She had known it was all going dreadfully wrong.

"I wanted to shake you, and say, 'Who are you and what the hell have you done with Jessica?'"

It wasn't until after he'd gone from her life that she realized how stupid it had been to make an issue out of the very things she then had missed.

"But you—" Jessica's defensive response died on her lips. She considered the possibility he was right. Instead of feeling defensive, she let what he had just said sink in. Suddenly, for the first time, it occurred to her maybe she should be the one who was sorry. If she was going to move on, if she was going to be a good parent—no, a great parent—to a child someday, she had to start working on herself now. And part of that meant facing her role in the relationship going wrong.

Up until this point, had she really told herself she had no part in it? That it was all his fault?

"What happened to you?" he asked. "And worse, what did I have to do with it?"

"Nothing," she said softly, and with dawning realization. "You had nothing to do with it. I think, Kade, ever since my mom died, I longed to have *that* world again.

"I was only twelve when she was diagnosed with a rare form of cancer. She went from diagnosis to dead in three weeks."

"I know that," he said, reminding her he knew so much about her.

"But what you didn't know—maybe what I didn't even know until this minute—was that I wanted my world back. After she died, it was just my dad and my brother and me. Everything went south. The house was a catastrophe. We ate takeout and macaroni and cheese. I couldn't even invite a friend over, our house was such a disaster. I wanted my lovely, stable family back."

"Oh, Jessie," he said. "I probably should have figured that out."

"And then we got married," she said slowly, "and I already had this idea in my head what a perfect life looked like, and I set out to make our life together look like that. And when I could sense you were dissatisfied, I thought it was because we needed to take the next step— to solidify ourselves as a family."

"You decided you wanted to have a baby."

"Didn't you want to have a baby?" she asked.

"Of course I did," he reassured her. "But maybe not for me. I wanted you to be happy. It didn't seem as though paint chips and the creative use of tarragon were making you happy. It certainly didn't seem as though I was making you happy."

CHAPTER SEVENTEEN

So HERE WAS a painful truth looking Jessica in the face. She'd had a wonderful husband who loved her, and somehow she had managed to manufacture misery.

Not that their challenges had not been real, but why hadn't she been able to focus on everything that was right and good, instead of working away at the tiny cracks until they had become fractures between Kade and her?

As painful as this conversation was, Jessica was relieved by it. This was the conversation they had needed to have a year ago, when everything had fallen apart so completely between them. Maybe if they had had it even before that, they could have stopped things from progressing to a complete fallout.

"When the first miscarriage happened," Jessica admitted softly, "I think it was a cruel reminder of what I'd already learned from my mother's illness—I was not in control of anything. And yet instead of surrendering to that, I fought it hard. The more out of control I felt, the more I started trying to control everything. Maybe especially you."

"Jessica," Kade said, and his voice was choked, "I always saw the failure as mine, not yours."

Her eyes filled with tears. It was not what she needed to hear, not right now, just as she was acknowledging her part in their marriage catastrophe.

"When I married you," Kade said, his voice low and pain-filled, "it felt as if that was a sacred vow and that I had found my lifelong duty. It was to protect you. To keep you safe. To stop bad things from happening. I felt as if my love should be enough to protect us—and you—from every storm.

"When it wasn't? When the growing chasm between us was made impassable by the two miscarriages, I could not enter your world anymore. I felt as if I was losing my mind. Those miscarriages, those lost babies, made me admit to myself how powerless I was. I couldn't do the most important thing I'd ever wanted to do. I could not save my own babies.

"And that compounded the fact I was already

dealing with a terrible sense of failure at lesser levels."

"What levels?" she asked.

"I had failed to even make you happy. I wanted you to stop trying to get pregnant. But you wouldn't. It made me feel as if I was not enough to meet your needs. It felt as if the bottom fell out of our whole world. When you wanted to keep trying—keep subjecting yourself and us to that roller-coaster ride of hope and joy and grief and despair—I just couldn't do it. And so I retreated to a world where I could be in control."

"And abandoned me," she whispered.

"Yes," he said quietly. "Yes. Yes, I did abandon you. But I think not nearly so thoroughly as you abandoned yourself. It was as if a baby was going to become your whole reason and your whole life."

She realized that she had not been ready then, and she was not really ready now, either. She began to cry. She had vowed no more losses, and now she faced the biggest one of all. Somehow in marriage, she had lost herself. She had become the role she played instead of the person she was.

Kade had always hated tears.

Always. If they argued and she started crying, he left.

Except when they had lost the first baby. They had crawled into bed together and clung to each other and wept until there were no tears left.

But after that, it was as if he steeled himself against that kind of pain, against feeling so intensely ever again. Even after the devastation of the loss of the second baby, he had been capable of only a few clumsy claps on the shoulder, a few of the kinds of platitudes she had come to hate the most.

It had seemed as if her grief had alienated him even more, had driven him away even more completely.

The tears trickled down her cheeks. She could not stop them now that they had been let loose.

She expected him to do what he had always done: escape at the first sign of a loss of control on her part. But he didn't.

"Jessie," Kade said softly. "In retrospect, we weren't ready for those babies. Neither of us was. We thought our relationship was on firm ground, but at the first stress, it fractured, so it wasn't. Babies need to come into a stronger place than that."

He came and he put his arms around her. He drew her deep against him, doing what she had needed so desperately from him all along. He let her tears soak into his shirt.

"I'm okay now," she finally sighed against him. "Thank you."

"For what?" he growled.

"For holding me. It's all I ever needed. Not for you to fix things, but for you to be there, as solid as a rock, when things went sideways."

He looked at her. He nodded. She could see the regret in his face. She could see that he got it. Completely.

And then something changed in his eyes, and he reached down and lifted a tear off her cheek with his finger, and scraped his thumb across her lip.

Jessica could feel the move into the danger zone. And she should have stepped back from it. But she could not.

A part of her that would not be controlled missed him—and missed this part of their life together—with a desperation that made her think she knew how heroin addicts felt. The *need* overshadowed everything. It overpowered common sense and reason. It certainly overpowered the need to be in control and the need to be right.

They were all gone—common sense and reason, control and the need to be right. They were gone, and in their place his thumb scraping across her lip became her whole world. Her lips parted, and she drew his thumb into her mouth. His skin tasted of heaven.

He went very still. She gazed up at him. And then she stood on her tiptoes, and she pulled his head down to her. She kissed that beautiful, familiar little groove behind his ear. He groaned his surrender and placed his hands on each side of her face and looked down at her, and then lowered his mouth to hers.

Welcome.

Welcome home.

His hunger was as apparent as hers. He crushed her lips under his own. His tongue found the hollow of her mouth, and she melted against him as he devoured her. His lips moved away from hers and he anointed the hollow of her throat and the tip of her nose and her eyelids.

"Jessica," he said hoarsely. "Oh, Jessica."

He scooped her up in his arms and went to the hallway to his bedroom. He tapped open the partially closed door with his foot, strode across the room and laid her on his king-size bed. It gave luxuriously under her weight. She stared up at him.

And wanted her husband, Kade, as she had never wanted anything else in her entire life. The wanting sizzled in her belly, and curled around her heart, and came out her lips as a moan of desire and invitation. She held out her good arm to him.

And he came willingly down to her, laying his body over hers, careful to hold his weight off her broken wing. He found the lobe of her ear and nipped it with delicate precision. He rained tiny kisses down on her brow and her nose and her cheeks and her chin.

Finally, when she was gasping with wanting and longing, he captured her lips and nuzzled teasingly. And then he took her lips more deeply, laying his claim, stoking the fire that was already there to white-hot.

"I am going to melt," she said hoarsely.

"Melt, then," he whispered. "Melt, and I will come with you."

His mouth on hers became a fury of possession and hunger. His tongue plunged the cool cavern of her mouth, exploring, darting, resting, tasting. He left her mouth and trailed kisses down the open collar of her shirt. He laid his trail of fire down her neck and onto her breastbone. His fingers found the buttons of her blouse and released them one by one. His lips found the nakedness of her flesh where it mounded above her bra, then blazed down the rise of her ribs to the fall of her belly. His lips went to all the places on her that only his lips had ever been before.

She did not melt. Rather, the heat built to a near explosion. The first of July, Canada Day, was weeks away, but the fireworks had begun already. They started, always, with the smaller ones, delightful little displays of color and noise, smoke and beauty. But they built and built and built to a fiery crescendo that lit the entire sky and shook the entire world.

It was obvious from the need that ached within her, from the way her body arched against him in welcome and anticipation, that this particular set of fireworks was heading toward only one possible climax.

"My arm— I don't know…" she whispered. It was her only uneasiness. She felt no guilt and no regret. He was her husband, and they belonged to each other in this way. They always had.

Kade took his weight off her and drank her in deeply.

"Do you want to do this?" he asked, and his voice was a rasp of raw need.

She knew her answer, her certainty, was in her face, and vibrating along the whole length of her body.

"I do. It's just with my arm like this, I don't know how we're going to manage," she said.

"I do," Kade whispered, his voice a growl of pure and sensual need. He had, intentionally or not, echoed their vows. *I do.* "Do you trust me, Jessie?"

"Yes."

"I know exactly how we are going to do this," he told her.

And he did. And so did she.

When they were done, in the sacred stillness that followed, the truth hit her and hit her hard.

It was not that she loved her husband again. It was that she had never stopped. Cradling the warmth of that truth to her, in the arms of her beloved, *home* for the first time in more than a year, Jessica slept.

Kade woke deep in the night. Jessica was asleep beside him, curled tightly against him, like a puppy seeking warmth. He felt tenderness toward her unfurl in him with such strength it felt as if his throat was closing. He'd known, in some deep place inside himself, ever since he'd seen the police cars in front of her store that morning, that he still loved her.

That he could not imagine a world without her. Not just *a* world. *His world.*

Something buzzed by his ear, and Kade realized it was that sound that had woken him up, and he was momentarily confused. His phone was automatically set to Do Not Disturb during the evening hours. He picked it up off the nightstand and squinted at it. It was four-thirty in the morning.

The phone buzzed again, vibrating in his hand. It was not his normal ring. Suddenly it occurred to him they had programmed the alarm at Baby Boomer to this phone to override his do-not-disturb settings. He unlocked the screen. Sure enough, there was a live-feed image of someone at the door of Baby Boomer.

Glancing at Jessica and seeing how peaceful she looked, Kade slipped from the bed, grabbed his clothes off the floor and went out into the hall. He called 911, with his phone tucked in against his ear, pulling on his pants at the same time. He explained what was happening, but the operator sounded particularly bored with his news of an alarm going off and a possible break-in in progress.

He thought of Jessica with her arm immobilized and he thought of her ongoing sleep disturbances and about the way she startled every time there was a loud sound. Even in the cubicle of the dress shop, when the music had started unexpectedly, she had nearly jumped out of her skin. Thinking of that, Kade felt really, really angry. Dangerously angry.

Jessica needed to know that he would look after her. That he would protect her. If her world was threatened, he would be there. He would put his body between her and a bullet if he had to.

And so, like a soldier getting ready to do battle for all he believed in, Kade went out the apartment door, got in his car and headed at full speed to her store.

At first it appeared no one was there. But then he noticed the newly repaired door hanging open and a sliver of light moving inside the store.

Without a single thought, he leaped from the car and took the stairs two at a time. He burst in the door and raced across the room and tackled the shadowy figure by the cash register.

Jessica was right. The thief was scrawny! Holding him in place was ridiculously easy. The anger at all the grief this guy had caused

Jessica seemed to seep out of him. The thief was screaming, "Please don't hurt me."

He seemed skinny and pathetic, and just as Jessica had guessed, desperate with a kind of desperation Kade did not know.

Kade heard sirens and saw flashing lights, and moments later the police were in the doorway, telling *him* to put his hands in the air. It seemed to take forever to sort it all out, but finally, he finished filling out reports and doing interviews.

It was now nearly seven. Jessica was probably awake and probably wondering where he was.

He called her, and could hear the anxiety in her voice as soon as she answered the phone.

"Where are you?"

"The alarm at your business alerted to my phone a couple of hours ago. I headed over here."

"*You* answered the alarm?"

"Well, I called the police, but I just wanted to make sure they caught him." He laughed, adrenaline still coursing through his veins. "You were right, Jessie. He was scrawny."

She cut him off, her voice shrill. "You caught the thief?"

"Yeah," he said proudly.

"But you are the one who lectured me about being foolhardy!"

He frowned. He wanted to be her hero. He wanted her to know her world was safe with him. Why didn't she sound pleased? Why wasn't she getting the message?

"You could have been killed," she said. "He could have had a gun or a knife. You're the one who pointed that out to me."

"Jessica, it all worked out, didn't it?"

"Did it?" she said, and he did not like what he heard in her voice. "Did it, Kade?"

"Yes!"

"Kade, being in a relationship means thinking about the other person."

"I *was* thinking about you."

"No, you weren't."

"How about if you don't tell me what I was thinking about? We had a great night last night. It doesn't mean you own me. It doesn't mean you get to control me. You know what this conversation feels like? *Here we go again.*"

"Does it?" she said, and her voice was very shrill. "Well, try this out—here we *don't* go again!"

And she slammed down the phone. He stared

at his phone for a long time, and finally put it back in his pocket. He already knew, when he got back to his apartment, she would be gone.

CHAPTER EIGHTEEN

JESSICA HUNG UP the phone. She was shaking violently. She hugged herself against the feeling of being cold.

And she faced an awful truth about herself. Her courage was all used up. She did not have one drop left. This love made her feel so vulnerable, and she did not want to feel that way anymore.

She thought of how it had been last night, of Kade's heated lips anointing every inch of her fevered flesh.

In the cold light of dawn, her heart swelled with loving him.

But it didn't feel good at all. It felt as if that love could not make her whole and could even destroy what was left of her.

It was her curse: her mother, whom she had loved so deeply, taken from her. And then each of those babies, whom she had loved madly and beyond reason, without even having met them, gone from this earth.

Loving Kade felt as if it was leaving herself open to one more loss. And he could be reckless. Impulsive. Look what he had just done! That could have been a far different phone call. It could have been the police calling to tell her Kade was dead.

Was he right? Was she trying to control him? Whatever—she had a deep sense that she could not sustain one more loss.

Quietly, Jessica walked through his beautiful apartment. With each step a memory: pizza and warm croissants and sitting on the sofa and playing a Scrabble game. She went back to the guest room, put on the nearest thing she could find, but left all the rest of the clothing they had bought together, because it, too, held too many memories.

Of dancing with him in Chrysalis. She should have recognized the danger right that second, before rickshaw rides, and Chinese food in the park, and falling asleep on a blanket with the trees whispering their names. Before it had all built to that moment last night of unbridled passion, of *hoping* for the most uncertain thing of all.

The future.

Feeling like a thief who had stolen the most precious thing of all, a moment of the pure pleasure of love, Jessica slipped out the door of Kade's empty apartment and locked it behind her. She went down to the lobby and had the concierge call her a cab.

In minutes, she was being whisked through the dawn-drenched city. As soon as they pulled up in front of her house, she wished that she had thought to go to a hotel.

Because this was more of them, of her and of Kade. It was the house they had chosen together and lived in together and loved in together.

And fought in together, she reminded herself, and watched love make that torturous metamorphosis to hate.

She could not survive that again. She could not survive losing him again.

When she let herself in the house, she felt relief. It wasn't really *their* house anymore. Though all her familiar furniture was back, except her bench, which was still in the back of a truck somewhere, everything else felt new.

Except Behemoth, which seemed to be squatting on the new floor glaring accusingly at her.

It even smelled new, of floor varnish and paint. The floors glowed with soft beauty; the walls had been painted a dove gray. The soot was gone from where they had tried to use the fireplace that one time, and it was gone off the ceiling.

Jessica went through to the kitchen, and it was as she had dreaded. She reached up and touched the cabinets. The oak stain was no longer bleeding through the white, and that, more than anything else, made her feel like crying.

She kicked off her shoes and passed her bedroom. There would be no going back to bed. She was sure of that. She went to her office and slid open the desk drawer.

Jessica took out all the documents she needed to start filling out to begin the adoption procedure, to get on with her dreams of a life in a way that did not involve him.

But as she stared at the papers, she realized she was terrified of everything that love meant, and especially of the built-in potential for loss and heartbreak.

She was not whole. She had never been whole. She had brought a neediness to her and Kade's relationship that had sucked the life out of it. And if she did not get herself sorted out, she would do the same to a child.

She thought of putting the documents back in the desk drawer, but it seemed to her they would be just one more thing to move, to sort through when the time came to leave here. It seemed to her she was not at all sure what she wanted anymore.

She dumped the papers in the garbage, and then she went and sat on the couch and hugged her knees to herself, and cried for who she was not, and what she was never going to have.

Finally, done with crying, done with Kade, done with dreams, she called the real estate office. An agent was there promptly, and Jessica calmly walked through the house with him as he did his appraisal. She felt numb and disconnected, as if the agent was on one side of a thick glass wall, and she was on the other. She didn't really care what price he put on the house. In fact, she barely registered the number he had given her. She gave him the listing, signed the papers, and he pounded the for-sale sign into her lawn.

She kept hoping her phone would ring, but it didn't. She and Kade had arrived at the same place, all over, an impasse that neither of them would be willing to cross. If it was a good thing, why did she feel so bereft?

After she had watched the agent pound the sign in in front of her house, she went outside and invited him to come by Baby Boomer and do the very same thing.

In the brutal light of this heartbreak, Jessica could see herself all too clearly. The business had risen from her neediness, from her need for something outside herself to fill her. It had been part of that whole obsession that she had not been able to let go of, not even after it had cost her her marriage to the man she loved.

Jessica expected to feel sad when the for-sale sign went up in front of Baby Boomer.

Instead, she felt relief. She felt oddly free.

It was going to be different now. She thought about what she really wanted, and she remembered when she had first met Kade, before she had lost herself, who she had been. An artist, not drawing pictures of bunnies on nursery walls, but drawing from a place deep within her.

That night, after she had closed the shop for the day, she went into the art-supply store next door. As soon as she walked in the door, the smells welcomed her—the smell of canvases and paints and brushes.

It smelled of home, she told herself firmly, her true home, the self she had walked away from again and again and again.

But home conjured other images: Kade laughing, and Kade with his feet up on the coffee table, and Kade's socks on the floor, and

Kade opening a box of pizza, and her sitting on a sander laughing so hard she cried. She shook that off impatiently.

She had made her vow, her new vow. And it was not to have and to hold. The vow she intended to obey was that she would not lose anything else. Not one more thing. And that meant not doing anything that would open her to loss.

Possibly more than any other single thing, loving Kade fell into that category.

Over the next weeks Jessica had to relearn a terribly hard lesson: you didn't just stop loving someone because you wanted to, because it had the potential to hurt you.

Love was always there in the background, beckoning, saying you can have a larger life if you risk this. But she thought maybe it was from living in the house they had shared together that she could not shake her sense of grief and torment.

Not even painting could fill her.

So she did other things she had always wanted to do and held back from. She signed up for a rock-climbing course, and a kayaking program, and a gourmet-cooking class. She had a sense of needing to fill every second so that she would not have time to think, to be drawn into the endless pool of grief that was waiting to drown her. Jessica was aware she was searching frantically to find things she could be passionate about that did not involve that sneaky, capricious, uncontrollable force called love.

But the more she tried to do, the more exhausted she became. If these efforts to fill her life were right, wouldn't she feel energized by them, instead of completely drained? At rock climbing, her limbs were so weak she could not hold herself on the wall. At kayaking—which was only in a local swimming pool for now—she fell out of the kayak and had a panic attack. At cooking class, she took one taste of her hollandaise sauce and had to run to the bathroom and be sick.

The feeling of weakness progressed. Jessica felt tired all the time. She had fallen asleep at work. She cried at the drop of a hat. Her stomach constantly felt as if it was knotted with anxiety.

Obviously, she had been absolutely correct when she had told him, "Here we *don't* go again." She took this as evidence that she was doing the right thing. If she was having this kind of reaction to a weeklong reunion with her husband, what would happen to her if they tried it for another year? Or two? And *then* it didn't work? Obviously, she could not survive.

"You need to go see a doctor," Macy said to her after finding her fast asleep, her head on her arms on her desk. "Something is wrong with you."

And so she went to see the doctor. She knew nothing was wrong with her. Love was not an ailment a doctor could cure. You could not take a pill to mend a broken heart. The doctor ordered a raft of tests, and Jessica had them all done, knowing nothing would come of it.

But then the doctor's office phoned and asked her to come back in. There were test results they needed to discuss with her in person.

And that was when she knew the truth. Jessica knew that, like her mother, she was sick and dying. Thank God she had not proceeded with her adoption idea. Thank God she had not proceeded with loving Kade.

It was just another confirmation that she could not allow herself to love. People could leave her, but she could leave people, too. It was all just too risky.

The doctor swung into the room, all good cheer. Jessica guessed he'd had a fantastic golf game that completely overrode the news he was about to give her.

She waited for him to remember the gravity of breaking it to someone that they were dying.

But that foolish grin never left his face!

"I have wonderful news for you," he said. "You're pregnant."

She stared at him. Life was too cruel. All those years of charts and temperatures and schedules, and now she was pregnant. Plus, she knew a terrible truth. Being pregnant did not necessarily mean walking away with a baby at the end.

Hadn't she decided she was unsuited for motherhood? She called Macy and told her she wouldn't be in for the rest of the day. She went home.

Her real estate agent was on the steps. "I've been trying to call you all morning. We have an offer on your house! A great offer."

Numbly she signed the paper he shoved at her. She went into the house and closed the door. Despite all her efforts to control everything, to keep change at bay, everything was changing anyway.

What was she going to tell Kade?

Nothing. He would feel trapped. He would feel as if he had to do the honorable thing, be sentenced to a life of bickering with her.

No. There had been no pretense in their last night together. He did love her. She knew that.

And now they were in the same place all over again. Where that love would be tested by life. What would make it different this time? If they lost another baby, how would it be any better this time?

"It won't," Jessica told herself. "It won't be better. It will be worse."

She lay down on the couch and cried and cried and cried. She hoped she had cried until there were no tears left, but from experience, she knew. There were always tears left. There was always an event waiting to blindside you, waiting to make you find that place where you had hidden a few extra tears.

CHAPTER NINETEEN

KADE DISCONNECTED FROM the phone call. He was part owner in his and Jessica's house, so he had been notified. It had just sold. Jessica, apparently, could not even tell him that herself. That had been a secretary at the real estate company asking him to come in and sign some documents.

He had not seen or heard from Jessica since that night when they had made love, and then he had made the fateful decision to go and tackle the breaking and entering at her business himself.

For a guy who thought he had the emotional range of a rock, he was stunned by how he felt.

Angry. And then sad. Frustrated. Powerless. And then sad some more.

He loved his wife. He loved her beyond reason. They were two intelligent people. Why could they not build a bridge across this chasm that divided them?

He mulled over the news about the house. What was he going to do now? Should he be the one to try to cross the minefield between them? A man had to have his pride.

But it seemed to Kade pride might have had quite a bit to do with why they could not work things out in the first place.

Maybe a man didn't have to have his pride.

Maybe a man having his pride really had nothing to do with being strong, with doing what needed to be done, with doing the right thing. Maybe a man had to swallow his pride.

Jessica, Kade knew, would never take the first step toward reconciliation, and for a second he felt angry again.

But then he relived her voice on the phone that morning of the break-in. It occurred to him that Jessica had not been trying to control him. She had been genuinely terrified.

Suddenly, he felt ashamed of himself. Wasn't this part of what was destroying them? Pride? Okay, it was a guy thing. It was always all about him. Even when he told himself it was about her. For example, he would go and save her store. But it had really been about him. He'd wanted to be the hero. He'd wanted to see her eyes glowing with admiration for him.

Maybe it was time for him to grow up.

To see things through her eyes, instead of through the warp of his own colossal self-centeredness.

She had been terrified.

And right from the beginning, from the day he had first seen her again, after she had tried to take out the thief herself at her store, she had given him clues where all that terror came from.

I lost my mother when I was twelve. I've lost two babies to miscarriage. I am not losing anything else. Not one more thing.

Kade had seen what losing those babies had done to her. He had seen the intensity of her own love tear her apart.

He had seen photos of her when she was a girl. In her fifth-grade class photo, she had been grinning merrily at the camera, all leprechaun charm and joyous mischief. But by the following year, when her mother had died, she had looked solemn and sad, the weight of the whole world on her shoulders.

He tried to imagine her at twelve, her sense of loss, her sense of the world being a safe place being gone.

The loss of each of those babies would have triggered that old torment, that sense of the world not being safe.

As would the man she loved putting himself at risk.

And suddenly, he despised himself. So what if she tried to control him?

"Kade," he said and swore to himself. "Don't you get it? It's not all about you."

He loved her. He loved Jessica Clark Brennan, his wife, beyond reason. He had cut her loose to navigate her heartbreaks on her own. When she had disappeared into that dark world of her own heartache, instead of having the courage to go in with her, to help her find her way back out, he had abandoned her.

That was not love.

But how was he going to make her see that he understood that now? He suspected she had spent the past weeks building up her defenses against him—against love. How was he going to knock them back down?

They had just sold a house together. The most natural thing in the world would be to bring a bottle of champagne over there and celebrate with her.

And it was time for honesty. Not pride. Pride

didn't want her to know how he felt, pride did not want to be vulnerable to her.

But love did. Love wanted her to know how he felt and love wanted to be vulnerable to her.

Pride had won throughout their separation.

Now it was time to give love, their love, a chance. A second chance.

With his mind made up, a half hour later, Kade knocked on the door of the house they had shared. He saw Jessica come to the window, and then there was silence. For a moment, he thought she was not going to open the door.

But then she did.

What he saw made him feel shattered. She was in one of those horrible dresses again. He thought she had been kidding about one being available in camo, but no, she hadn't been. Aside from the horror of the dress, Jessica looked awful—tired and pale and thin.

"Hello, Jessica," he said quietly. His voice sounded unnatural to him.

"Did you come to get your check?"

"My check?" he asked, genuinely confused. Obviously there would be no money yet from a house that had barely sold.

"I told you I'd pay you for those clothes from Chrysalis once the house sold."

"You didn't even take the clothes with you."

"What? Are you wearing them?"

"Are you crazy?"

"Because if you're not, I'm paying for them."

"Okay," he said. "I am, then. Wearing them."

Just a glimmer of a smile, before she doused it like a spark of a fire in a tinder-dry forest. Still, despite her look of studied grimness, was there a shadow of something in her eyes? Something that she did not want him to see? Despite all her losses, and despite the fact she wanted not to, he could tell she *hoped*.

And her hope, to him, was the bravest thing of all.

"Well, then, did you bring back my bench?"

"No."

"What are you doing here, then?"

"Isn't it obvious? I brought a bottle of champagne. I thought we should celebrate the sale of our house."

"Oh."

"This is the part where you invite me in," he told her gently.

"What if I don't want you to come in?" she said.

But he could still see that faint spark of hope in her eyes.

"We still have some business to complete,

Jessie." Ah, she'd never been able to resist him when he called her Jessie.

She stood back from the door, her chin tilted up in defiance of the hope he had seen in her eyes. He went in.

He tried to hide his shock at what he found inside the house. The house was not a reflection of Jessica. And it wasn't just that the floors had been refinished, either. There were things out of place. There was a comforter and a pillow on the sofa. Empty glasses littered the coffee table. There were socks on the floor.

Really? It was all very frightening. "Are you okay?" he asked her.

She went and sat down on the sofa, crossed her arms over her chest in defense. Against him. "I'm fine. What do you want to discuss?"

"Ah." He went through to the kitchen with his bottle of wine. "How's your arm?" he called. Maybe that was the explanation for the mess. She was not completely able-bodied.

"It's okay. The cast has been off for a bit. I have some exercises I do to strengthen my muscles."

The corkscrew was in a familiar place. How was it this kitchen felt so much more like home than his own masterpiece of granite and stainless steel? He opened the bottle, got glasses down and poured. He hated it that the cabinets had been fixed.

He went back and handed her a wineglass, and sat down beside her. He noticed the black soot stain up the front of the fireplace had been fixed, too.

It was as if their memories were being erased, one by one. "Here's to the sale of the house," he said.

"To moving on," she agreed hollowly. But she set her glass down without taking a sip.

He took a sip of his own wine, watching her carefully over the rim of his glass. A bead of perspiration broke out over her lip, and her face turned a ghastly shade of white.

He set his glass down and reached for her, afraid she was going to tumble off the sofa. "Jessica?"

She slid away from his touch and found her feet. She bolted for the bathroom, and didn't even have time to shut the door. The sound of her getting violently sick filled the whole house.

No wonder the place was a wreck. She wasn't feeling well.

She came back into the room, looking weak and wasted. She sat on the couch, tilted her head against the back and closed her eyes.

"Why did you say you were fine? Why didn't you just tell me you had the flu?"

"Sorry," she mumbled. "I should have told you. I don't want you to catch anything."

Her eyes were skittering all over the place. She was a terrible liar. She had the same look on her face right now that she'd had the year she'd denied buying him the golf clubs he'd wanted for a long time, when she really had.

But why would she lie about having the flu? Or maybe the lie would be that she didn't want him to catch anything.

He looked at her hard. After a long time, she looked back at him, proud and…right beneath that, what? *Scared?* Of what? Him?

Kade felt a strange stillness descend on him, the kind of stillness you might feel in a church with sun pouring through a stained glass window.

He *knew.* He knew right to the bottom of his soul. Jessica was pregnant. He was being given a second chance.

She looked away. "Yeah," she finally said, the word obviously an effort from the lie inherent to it. "The flu."

"Uh-huh."

Her eyes flew to his face, then moved away again.

"You're pregnant, aren't you, Jessica?"

She was silent for a bit and then she sighed with a kind of relief. "Imagine that," she said quietly. "All those charts and temperatures and schedules, all that taking all the fun out of it, and then one night. One single night…"

"Are you happy at all?" he asked her quietly.

"It's pretty hard to be happy when you're terrified," she said. "You know what the cruelest irony is, Kade? I'd just realized, with your help, that I am not ready for a baby!"

It came out very close to a wail of pure panic.

"Aw, Jess," he said quietly, "maybe that *is* when you are ready. When you can see your own imperfections and embrace them. Maybe it's when you can see it's an imperfect world, and instead of trying to impose perfection on it, you just embrace that, too. Maybe that's the only real lesson we can give a baby. It's the one I learned from the failure of us. The world is not going to be perfect. Life is not going to be easy. I can't control everything. But together, with love for each other, we can handle whatever it throws at us."

"We?" she whispered.

"Jessie, I am not leaving you alone with this. And maybe that's what I really wanted to say that night when you told me you were planning to adopt a baby. Not that you weren't ready, or that you had issues to work on, because who could ever be ready for a baby? And who does not have issues to work on? I guess what I was trying to say that night was that it's a lot to take on alone. I didn't want to think about you taking it on without me. It's going to take two people, stumbling through, to bring this baby into the world.

"I'm going to be there for you this time."

Her eyes went to his face, and this time they stayed there, wide and hopeful. She wanted to believe—the capacity for hope was there—but she was frightened, too. And who could blame her?

"I know my track record stinks," he said.

She didn't disagree with that.

"And I know I can't protect you from life. Or from loss. I know we're months away from holding a baby in our arms, and I know you're scared this is going to end like all the other times. All I can really protect you from is walking through difficult times alone."

She was crying now.

"Jessica, I've been given a second chance to be a better man. And I'm taking it. I'm proving to you—and to myself—that I can live up to those vows we took. I remember those vows. I remember each word of them. So listen to me. Because I'm doing this again. And I'm doing it right this time."

His voice was hoarse with emotion, almost a whisper at first, and then with it growing stronger and stronger, he spoke.

"I, Kade Brennan, take you, Jessica, to be my wife, my heart and my soul, my companion through life and my one and only love. I will cherish you and I will nurture a friendship based in trust and honor. I will laugh with you and, especially, I will cry with you. I will love you faithfully, today, tomorrow and forever. Through the best and the worst, through the difficult and the easy, whatever may come, I will always be there for you. I have given you my hand." Kade held out his hand to her, cleared his throat and said, "I have given you my hand to hold, and so I give also my life into your keeping."

To him, it seemed like forever that she looked at him, her eyes sparkling with unshed tears. And then her hand slipped into his, as if it had never left it, as if this was where her hand was meant to be.

Jessica spoke. Her voice was husky and tears were set free and flowed down her face, just as they had that day all those years ago, when he had cherished her tears instead of seeing them as a sign of his own powerlessness.

She said, "I, Jessica Clark-Brennan, take you, Kade, to be my husband, my heart and my soul, my companion in life and my one and only true love. I will cherish you and I will nurture our friendship, based in trust and honor. I will laugh with you, and, yes, I will cry with you. I will love you faithfully, today, tomorrow and forever. Through the best and the worst, through the difficult and the easy, whatever may come, I will always be there. I have given you my hand to hold, and so I give also my life into your keeping."

She had her knuckles in her eyes, scrubbing like a child who just wanted the tears to go away.

But that was their past. Her tears had upset him and made him feel helpless and hopeless, and so he had turned away. And so she had begun to try to hide how she felt from him, the very one she should have been able to lean on, the one she should have been able to be completely transparent and completely herself with.

Not this time. This time he was walking right into the fire. He slid over on the sofa and crossed the small space that remained between them. Gently, he scooped her up and put her on his lap. She did not resist. She sighed against him as if she had waited her whole life for this moment.

To feel safe, to feel looked after, to feel as if there was a slight possibility everything would be okay. He tucked her head into his shoulder, and felt her tears soak through his shirt.

It wasn't until a long time later that he realized that it was not only her tears soaking his shirt. His own, locked inside him for way too long, had joined hers.

He could not know how this pregnancy would end. But he did know, however it concluded, they were in this together this time. For all time.

"I love you," he said. "Jessie, I love you."

And then he held his breath.

Until he heard the words he needed to hear.

"Kade, I love you."

At that precise moment, the sound of her voice and her words washed over him, and he felt like a desert that had not seen rain for the longest time. He felt as if the moisture had come, fallen on the parched place that was his soul. He could feel the color and the life seeping back into his world.

CHAPTER TWENTY

"Hey, I like it."

"The dress?" Jessica said, turning to Kade. She was teasing. She knew he hated this dress, and every dress from her Poppy Puppins collection. But it did great as a paint smock, and it covered her growing girth beautifully. Jessica watched him shrug out of his jacket at the door.

"Of course not that dress." He wrinkled his nose. "I have to find your secret cache of those dresses. Every time I throw one out, three more appear."

She laughed. It was the small things that she had come to love the most: him coming through the door at night, playing a Scrabble game together, watching TV and eating popcorn together, him licking her fingers, slick with butter.

Sometimes she wondered, if they had never had a bad spell, if she had never known what it was like to live without him as part of her daily life, would she love these little things as much as she did? Would she have known to appreciate them?

She had moved into his place at River's Edge after her house had been turned over to the new owners. Eventually, after the baby was born, they would buy a house for the three of them.

But at the moment, they were both cautious about making decisions based on a baby. This caution remained, even though her due date was looming large. They didn't even have a nursery, and the guest room was untouched. No lavender paint or murals this time. No crib, no mobiles, no teddy bears.

They had a beautiful handmade crate they could line with blankets and put beside their bed. When the time came. She loved the idea of the baby sleeping next to them, so close they could breathe in each other's breath, exchange air, become even more a part of one another.

Kade came over and put his hand on the gentle swell of her belly under the paint smock.

He put his head down and spoke directly to her stomach. "Hello, baby. Do you hear me in there? Moving," he said with satisfaction. "A football player."

"Or a ballerina."

"Nah, it's a boy."

It was only in the past few weeks that they had dared to play this game, so afraid were they of jinxing this incredibly magical and miraculous experience. But this time, the fear was different. They would lie awake with it, deep into the night, holding hands, leaning on each other.

They had chosen not to know the sex of their child. This baby was a miracle, boy or girl. Besides, it was endlessly fun debating it, even as they carefully avoided the baby sections of the stores. It was like a superstition, but she did not care. She was not buying one thing for that baby until she had held it in her arms.

She had barely set foot in Baby Boomer since selling it to Macy. But she knew Macy had her covered. She knew there was a shelf there filled with things Macy was quietly selecting for her: bottles and blankets and tiny disposable diapers and little outfits. *If* the time came this time—that hope fluttered in Jessica's chest, they were so close now, and the doctor smiled and shook his head at Jessica's fears—they had a whole nursery that could be put in a box and delivered to them.

There was an unexpected new dimension to Jessica's relationship with Macy and with her old place of business.

Macy was selling paintings almost as fast as Jessica could produce them. Jessica was working largely in abstract, the colors and motion flowing out of her like rivers of light. It was as if this part of her, dammed up for too long, was bursting forth now that it had been set free.

And for some reason, that kind of art appealed to people shopping for baby stuff, not for nurseries, necessarily, though there was a whole move away from the cute traditional look of babies' rooms.

No, people having babies these days, and especially the ones who shopped at an upscale store like Baby Boomer, were largely established professional couples. They had whole gorgeous big houses to decorate, not just nurseries.

And the name Jessica Brennan was causing a surprising stir in the Calgary art scene.

"I like it," Kade said. Having greeted the baby, he turned his attention to the canvas. "What's it called?"

She didn't have a studio. The light pouring through the windows of his apartment had proved perfect. When it was too strong, she closed the curtains and had lights set up to point to the canvas. Between the canvases, paints, lights and paint tarps on the floor, the place looked very messy. Add to that a sock of Kade's, menus out on the counter and magazines on the coffee table, and the effect was one of moderate disarray. And she loved it.

Kade had, with gentle strength, helped her probe the origins of that terrible need to feel in control.

Perhaps, she thought, eyeing their space, she had gone a little too far the other way.

She lifted her shoulder. *Oh, well.*

She turned her attention to the canvas. She was not sure where this came from, this endless current of inspiration, but she was pretty sure it came from love.

"Today it's called *Joy Rising*." She shrugged. "Who knows if it will still be called that tomorrow."

"Joy Rising," Kade said, and stood back from it.

The backdrop of the canvas was a light gray neutral. The rest of it was filled with hundreds of bubbles—like soap bubbles—rising, starting small at the bottom left of the canvas, growing larger at they reached the right-hand corner.

"It's good," he said. "Now, what's for dinner?"

It was a standing joke between them, a light tease about what she liked to call her Martha Stewart phase. "The pizza menu is on the counter."

He laughed.

And his laughter shivered along her spine. They had almost lost this. They had almost walked away from it. And that was what made it even more precious today.

And maybe that was what all loss did, if you were brave, if you were open to its lessons. Maybe all loss sharpened your sense of the now, of the gifts of this very moment.

He had moved over and was studying the menu.

"Kade?"

"Huh?"

Jessica put her hand to her swollen belly. "Ah."

He was at her side in an instant, scanning her face.

"It's time," she said. "Oh, my God, it's time."

And even this moment, with intense ripples of pain possessing her body, was awash with light, with joy rising. Jessica looked into the face of the man who was her husband, and she read the strength there and knew, together, whatever happened next, it would be just fine.

Kade woke up. His neck was sore. He had fallen asleep in the chair. For a moment, he was disoriented, but then he heard a little sound, like a kitten mewing, and it all came back to him.

His eyes adjusted to the dark, and there they were. His wife and his daughter, the baby on Jessica's chest.

He had thought over the past few months with Jessica as they came together as a couple again, as they celebrated their second chance, that he had come to know the depth and breadth of love completely.

Now, looking at his child, he knew he had only kidded himself. He had only scratched the surface of what love could be.

The baby made that mewing sound again.

Jessica stirred but did not wake.

Jessica. How could someone that tiny, someone who appeared that fragile, be so damned brave? Men thought they were courageous, but that was only until they'd seen a baby born. And then they had to admit how puny their strength was, how laughable this thing they had passed off as courage was.

Courage certainly was not tackling a thief!

Kade got up from his chair. Jessica needed to rest. She had done her bit. Thirteen hours of the most unbelievable pain Kade could imagine.

How he had wanted to take that pain from her, to take her place.

But that was one of the lessons of this remarkable second chance. He could not take her pain away. He could not fix everything, or really, even most things.

He had to be there. He had to stand there in his own helplessness, and not run from it. He had to walk with her through her pain, not try to take it away from her. Admitting his own powerlessness sometimes took more courage than anything he had ever done before.

The baby mewed again, and stirred again.

He touched the tiny back of his baby girl. It was warm beneath his fingers. He could feel the amazing miracle of the life force in that tiny little bundle.

He had been the first to hold her, the nurse showing him how. He had looked into that tiny wrinkled face, the nose crunched and the eyes screwed tightly shut in outrage, and he had recognized her.

Love.

Love manifest.

And so, summoning his courage, he lifted the baby off the gentle rise and fall of his wife's sleeping chest.

He could hold her in the palm of one hand, his other hand supporting her neck, as the nurse had shown him.

Destiny.

They had decided to call her Destiny.

Her eyes popped open, a slate gray that the nurse had told him would change. They didn't know yet if she would have green eyes like Jessica's or blue like his, or some amazing combination of both.

The nurse had said, too, that this little baby probably could not see much.

And yet, as Kade held her, her eyes seemed to widen with delighted recognition.

"That's right, sweetie, it's me. Daddy."

Daddy. The word felt incredibly sweet on his tongue, and the baby squirmed in his hand. He drew her close to his chest and went and sat back down on the chair, awkwardly stroking her back.

He was so aware of how tiny she was, and helpless. How she was relying on him.

He felt a moment's fear. The world always seemed to be in such a fragile state. The weather changed and wars broke out, and floods came and fires.

People could be fragile, too, held in the trance of long-ago hurts, hiding the broken places within them.

There was so much that he was powerless

over, and yet this little girl would see him as all-powerful. Her daddy.

This was what he needed to teach her: that yes, the world could be fragile and easily broken. And people could be fragile and easily broken, too.

But there was one thing that was not fragile, and that was not easily broken.

And that thing was love.

It was the thread that ran, strong, through all the rest. It was what gave strength when strength failed, what gave hope when it was hopeless, what gave faith when there was plenty of evidence that it made no sense at all to have faith. It was what healed the breaks, and made people come out of the trance and embrace all that it was to be alive.

"Welcome to this crazy, unpredictable, beautiful, amazing life," Kade whispered to his little girl. "Welcome."

He closed his eyes, and when he opened them, Jessica's hand was on his shoulder, and she was awake, looking at them both.

"I need to confess something to you," Kade growled.

"What?"

"I've broken one of my vows to you."

"Impossible," she whispered.

"No. You are not my one and only true love anymore. I have two of you now."

And the smile on Jessica's face—radiant, a smile that shamed the very sun—said it was worth it. Every piece of pain they had navigated was worth it.

Because it had brought them here.

To this place. To this moment.

Where they knew that all else might pass away, but that love prevailed.

* * * * *

LARGER-PRINT BOOKS!

GET 2 FREE LARGER-PRINT NOVELS PLUS
2 FREE GIFTS!

HARLEQUIN®

Romance

From the Heart, For the Heart

YES! Please send me 2 FREE LARGER-PRINT Harlequin® Romance novels and my 2 FREE gifts (gifts are worth about $10). After receiving them, if I don't wish to receive any more books, I can return the shipping statement marked "cancel." If I don't cancel, I will receive 4 brand-new novels every month and be billed just $5.09 per book in the U.S. or $5.49 per book in Canada. That's a savings of at least 15% off the cover price! It's quite a bargain! Shipping and handling is just 50¢ per book in the U.S. and 75¢ per book in Canada.* I understand that accepting the 2 free books and gifts places me under no obligation to buy anything. I can always return a shipment and cancel at any time. Even if I never buy another book, the two free books and gifts are mine to keep forever.

119/319 HDN GHWC

Name _____ (PLEASE PRINT)

Address _____ Apt. #

City _____ State/Prov. _____ Zip/Postal Code

Signature (if under 18, a parent or guardian must sign)

Mail to the **Reader Service:**
IN U.S.A.: P.O. Box 1867, Buffalo, NY 14240-1867
IN CANADA: P.O. Box 609, Fort Erie, Ontario L2A 5X3

Want to try two free books from another line?
Call 1-800-873-8635 or visit www.ReaderService.com.

* Terms and prices subject to change without notice. Prices do not include applicable taxes. Sales tax applicable in N.Y. Canadian residents will be charged applicable taxes. Offer not valid in Quebec. This offer is limited to one order per household. Not valid for current subscribers to Harlequin Romance Larger-Print books. All orders subject to credit approval. Credit or debit balances in a customer's account(s) may be offset by any other outstanding balance owed by or to the customer. Please allow 4 to 6 weeks for delivery. Offer available while quantities last.

Your Privacy—The Reader Service is committed to protecting your privacy. Our Privacy Policy is available online at www.ReaderService.com or upon request from the Reader Service.

We make a portion of our mailing list available to reputable third parties that offer products we believe may interest you. If you prefer that we not exchange your name with third parties, or if you wish to clarify or modify your communication preferences, please visit us at www.ReaderService.com/consumerchoice or write to us at Reader Service Preference Service, P.O. Box 9062, Buffalo, NY 14240-9062. Include your complete name and address.

She stopped, close enough that she could almost feel his
breath on her face, but still not touching. Violet looked up
into his eyes and saw the control there. He was holding
back. So she wouldn't.

Bringing one hand up to rest against his chest, she felt
the thump of his heart through his shirt and knew she
wanted to be close to that beat for as long as he'd let her.
Slowly, she rose up onto her tiptoes, enjoying the fact that
he was tall enough that she needed to. And then, without
breaking eye contact for a moment, Violet kissed him.

It only took a moment before he responded, and Violet
let herself relax into the kiss as his arms came up to hold
her close. The celebrity wedding melted away, and all she
knew was the feel of his body against hers and the taste
of him on her lips. This. This was what she needed. Why
had she denied herself this for so long?

And how could it be that kissing Tom somehow tasted
like trust?

Eventually, though, she had to pull away. Tom's arms

kept her pressed against him, even as she dropped down to her normal height, looking up into his moss-green eyes.

"Is this where I give you some kind of line about getting to know me even better?" Tom asked, one eyebrow raised.

Violet's laugh bubbled up inside her, as if kissing Tom had released all the joy she'd kept buried deep down. "I think it probably is, yes."

"In that case, how long do you think we need to stay at this party?"

"There's five hundred people here," Violet pointed out. "What are the chances of them missing just two?"

"Good point." And with a warm smile spreading across his face, Tom grabbed Violet's hand and they ran for the waiting car.

Don't miss this enchanting conclusion to the
***SUMMER WEDDINGS** trilogy,*
FALLING FOR THE BRIDESMAID.
Available June 2015 wherever
Harlequin® Romance books and ebooks are sold.

www.Harlequin.com